Emergency

Also by Kathleen Alcott

America Was Hard to Find
Infinite Home
The Dangers of Proximal Alphabets

Emergency

STORIES

◆

Kathleen Alcott

W. W. NORTON & COMPANY
Celebrating a Century of Independent Publishing

For information about permission to reproduce selections from this book, write to Permissions, W. W. Norton & Company, Inc., 500 Fifth Avenue, New York, NY 10110

For information about special discounts for bulk purchases, please contact W. W. Norton Special Sales at specialsales@wwnorton.com or 800-233-4830

Manufacturing by Lakeside Book Company
Book design by Patrice Sheridan
Production manager: Julia Druskin

ISBN: 978-1-324-05188-6

W. W. Norton & Company, Inc.
500 Fifth Avenue, New York, N.Y. 10110
www.wwnorton.com

W. W. Norton & Company Ltd.
5 Carlisle Street, London W1D 3BS

1 2 3 4 5 6 7 8 9 0

For Annabel Davis-Goff, whose many lives
would shame a great man's one.
What haven't you given me? I love you,
I revere you, I thank you.

♦

Every garden is a replica, a representation, an attempt to recapture something, but the form it finds for the act is that of a mental picture. . . . We replace the world with our ideas of it, gardens being intermediate enough to make us think they are nature and not simply embellishments or enhancements of it, regions which unlike paintings let us forget there is anything beyond.

—ROBERT HARBISON, *ECCENTRIC SPACES*

If God exists he has no rival. Hell is our ambition for evil.

—VIOLETTE LEDUC, *LA BÂTARDE*

CONTENTS

✦

Emergency

EMERGENCY

◆

Whether she passed for a teenager, the summer she was thirty and the divorce went through, was not our concern. She did sit on those rocks above the river, as we heard it, did accept their cans of beer and drags of weed. We spoke of it in the same restaurants, the glasses at noon filling with green light from the park across the way, where she had once joined us. Toward the end, it must be said, we paid her check. We took those calls, to a point.

She had lived, for many years, on the kind of New York block you walk down in envy. All spring the old elm trees reach for each other, and in winter the stoops narrow by margins of white. On these streets there are houses whose curtains stay parted, the lighting fixtures on and children's books face-down on couches, and there is no greater sign of wealth, or of safety. Her name was Helen Tiel.

———

Helen's husband, ex, could not be blamed, although it was clear, from the way she spoke his name, that we were meant to see this as the origin of all—as if he had invented her, as if she had nothing to do with what her life had become, sublets and credit card debt, an evening on a drug meant for people five years younger that left her hearing off, she claimed, for weeks. His life since their marriage was obscure to her, something no two a.m. search term could mediate—a new younger woman, an apartment in Lisbon, though he kept the brownstone where they had thrown those dinners. She was a gifted host, you would have agreed. Rosemary threaded through lemons in the water pitcher, linen napkins beveled on the teak. After salmon tagine and mousse, you might go down to see what she was painting—her shows were written up, her gallerist was a good one. Helen's studio was bright, it gave onto the garden, and she kept those glass doors open. His Danish family had been rich for centuries, and the prenup was punitive. When she left the city, after an unhappy year alone, we agreed it was a good thing: some rented farmhouse in Maine, the calligraphy set, a shirt she wore—men's, striped and collared, buttoned low on her boyish chest. She sang to the chickens, she swam every day.

Helen had charisma, every email was clever, and the man whose place it was, his name was maybe Allan, had loaned her a car. He was a stranger from a listserv, but he had picked her up from the bus stop and showed her how to collect eggs before taking off in his truck. Soon she was posting all the time, gaining more followers, the river, the mesh porch where she had dragged the futon. The White Mountains where she hiked too far alone, a chevron hen with a sexual walk. She said, in a text to the tidiest one of us, that it was strange to stay in so cluttered a house: he had not done any of the things one might expect, emptied the refrigerator or the closets, and it was as if he wanted her to spy. In a phone call to another shortly after, she said he was something like the father she did not have. A sculptor, eccentric, his eyebrows longer than wide, his hands still very good with the fine parts of life. He was a few months from seventy and wore a turquoise ring. Behind the crazy garden—bulbous, mutant tomatoes, stalks of kale and sunflowers as tall as Helen—were treehouses he had built for his daughters. Even his wedding albums he had left out, and she mentioned how they moved her, everyone who loved the couple watching them through binoculars as they canoed away from the reception. Helen had no family (father dead, mother unreachable) but that she traced so much back to this seemed to leave something out. It came up too often, a rule in a game of make-believe that not all the children have agreed to, and that governs only its inventor.

Swimming became, for her, something like worship, a mile a day, three—then she began to go in the dark. Even health she treated unhealthfully. She liked how it was problem and solution, what made her sweat the same as what cleansed her. It was, this river, remarkable, as clean as it was jade, two fathoms deep in every direction, the trees on either side bending from the rocks like mothers. To swim in the hour before midnight was to be the same color as everything else: that was how she dramatically captioned a photo, a night she ignored two of our calls.

Allan was calling often, the reasons invented as he spoke,

their justification thinner as he drove farther away. Had she seen a mug, which he thought he had packed. Was she feeling safe, sleeping there alone, had she heard the bear, did she need the number of a neighbor. *I think you're a special person*, he texted, from the road trip he'd called spiritual: *I think what you're doing is brave*. Each afternoon she drove his car two miles to the same trailhead, where she hiked in her suit to the place she liked to swim. The boys set up every day just opposite her, the farthest you could go before the river widened and the wooded land on either side dropped to marsh. Halfway up a tree that leaned into the wind, on the stump of a branch, her shorts and shirt billowed as she swam. Her routine was across and back four times, a break to float if she needed that.

Of course she came to recognize them: the one whose earring winked as he jumped, the one who shotgunned Pabst without so much as a shudder in the bare curve of his spine. Another, tawny blond, seemed rarely to sit, disappearing often into the copse of hemlocks, reemerging to issue a punch line and run toward a perfect dive. To imagine their bedrooms took no effort, their rivalries or feats. The posters fallen from one corner, the labrador dyed purple, the fences hopped in escape from the broken-up party. They passed the first two weeks in wordless proximity as she swam toward then away, the boys' faces hung in sunlight between the violent peaks of their knees. Maybe she didn't want their desire, only to know she was not exempt from it.

The first day they waved, as she touched their side of the river, she laughed as if to communicate there had been some mistake. The second time, placing one hand on a branch that curved underwater, panting a little, having swum more quickly that day, she only nodded. Hey, yellow, the diver yelled, a reference to her suit, Italian, ruched in a small blossom between her breasts. He had scrambled halfway down. The can might have hit her, had it not been pitched so delicately. It floated just before her. It glowed a little.

Was it her feelings about the past—that it had been over too quickly—or the future—that it was coming too slowly—that made her do what she did next? Her ass on a submerged shelf, she tipped the can back and emptied it in one go, certain of their watching, then tossed it back to the boy, who had come closer, grinning from his crouch. Then she swam back across. With her back to the river, she pulled her shorts over her suit. They yelled something, as she buttoned her shirt, and over her shoulder she gave a grabby kind of wave.

———

At twenty-two Helen Tiel had been beautiful enough that her airfare was often covered, her presence in a room something that rearranged chairs. She had believed in her own essence—a potency that men loved, and might dilute for their purposes, but which replenished itself, and which she could afford to share. She was calling us weeping by twenty-eight, imagining that in passing down the street she elicited fewer looks and shouts, that strangers' hands might not open doors the moment she moved toward them. Around that time, at a dinner Helen was late for, seconds before she sallied through the door in a silk dress and wood bangles, the college friend among us pointed out the problem: it was like Helen thought she deserved beauty, that it was the product of her very own mind. Yes, we agreed. Of course we remembered when life opened that way—the walks home from school, crossing the street to avoid the voices of men or be closer to them. The world was lit by another source, those years told us, with a kind of excoriating malice from underneath, and we were more or less glad when that light started to go.

Her marriage was not yet over, but it must have progressed to the point that in the evenings she watched for his shadow in the square of light under the bedroom door, and took fearful message from whether it paused there or passed too easily up to his study. He was a biographer, eighteen years her senior, and worked on a typewriter he pounded in that room right above her. She had joked, at the dinners we ate by her poppy bed in his garden, that because he had not had sex until university he could not have been her father. He worked slowly and religiously on the lives of others, scrutinizing their childhoods, their habits and letters, taking notes until he established captious authority on their natures. Helen's life was no exception, and she was for a long time captivated by his sense of her facture. He knew how she was made, and of what, and he even seemed to know why. I was waiting for you, and we go together, he said in Danish, and had her parrot it until the delivery was right. If he became cruel in his way—wincing if she kissed him, counting how often she cried, saying he would not respond if she exceeded a certain monthly frequency—she was crazy in hers, and unlucky above it. Helen could not sleep, and she could not really work, saying when we asked why that her paintings had promise, but not execution. We knew that was wrong, and we knew it was a criticism that came from him. Once she sprained a wrist the same year she broke an ankle, and he told her, in the emergency room, fingers pinched to his nose, she had a certain: what was it: violence in the world. That indictment we could more or less confirm—when she repeated it, we were silent.

———

In the gravel turnout where she'd parked by the river, she was pulling out onto the road, just beginning to accelerate, when the earringed boy appeared before her, miming having been hit, twirling in the air with a tongue way out. There was laughter in the bushes, from which the diver appeared, hair in his face, electronic fog pouring from his mouth. Barefoot, sunglasses, a five-button fly. He approached her window with his phone out and handed it over, instructing she put in her number. Helen typed the numbers quickly, and didn't look his way as she pulled onto the road. Her phone was rattling in the cupholder before the eight-minute drive back was over.

what's up

we've been talking about you sooooo much lol

you don't go to school around here

Was it a question? Was this the moment to make things right or had it already passed, back in the car, back in the river with the beer in her hand, back in the early darkness of her marriage when she should have known she was replaceable, the way he started to close his eyes when she spoke? Those thin dresses she wore, things that looked like a spill, and how she pressed them into his leather-patched cardigans: it's easy to say she was stupid to believe it, but isn't it a nice idea, love coming late into someone's life like that, a bachelor at forty-something only by accident? The point is, we can all agree it's clear, that she basically believed those years were null and void, that age had not accrued. Next to him, next to his friends who often asked her birth year as a party trick, clapping the others' shoulders in shock, she had always been so young. She told us as much, how she had once truly forgotten, mentioned the wrong number to the doctor, given the age she had been the year she met her husband. Twenty-three. She'd gone in for a sinus infection, something that alarmed her more, the lawyer among us thought, than seemed rational. Helen called from urgent care at ten-thirty on a Tuesday, tearful and gasping, saying even her teeth hurt, saying she was scared of the yellow of her mucus.

Some of us rooted for the marriage longer, hoping for her sake that the unhappiness she described was balanced by a real commitment she elided. But ultimately, he was so clearly the type, a string of girls before her who also took the lessons in Danish he paid for, also fell in love with his aging relatives during summers in Odense. They all moved in quickly and ended up with the same haircut, a sort of androgynous bob he preferred, and which Helen, to her credit, refused. That she didn't put it together sooner: some of us thought it was arrogance. She was as smart as any of us, had read the second-wave feminist canon and had opinions about what had been excluded from the third. Perhaps the difference was something other than pride, sadder, more secular and more American. Helen still believed in a notion we had all worked to disavow, as all adults must: that to any rule, she might prove the brilliant exception.

———————

Wasn't there a moment when she considered blocking that boy's number? Helen walked into the house through the back way, the screen door on the mesh veranda slamming behind her, and stepped out of her pea-green Keds without untying them, her jeans without picking them up. On the futon where she starfish-flopped she stared at her phone. The room as she'd rearranged it was the dream of a little girl, a crocheted hammock chair hung in the corner, tea lights gripping everything, vases of flowers on the two wooden trunks she had dragged out to make bedside tables. Allan had offered his bedroom, which she had declined. She was stubborn about sleeping on the porch, even when it stormed, insisting it was vivifying to be that warm near something so wet. That she could hear the rooster when she woke, she said, made her feel close to sleepers across time. Observations like these indicated a certain state, one of us in therapy said, a speculative quality that seemed slightly manic.

She typed the reply quickly.

I live in New York.

She was trying to be direct—no opening, no invitation. He was eighteen, she thought.

doing a lot of swimmin in a lil yellow suit for somebody who lives in ny

come thru tomorrow for hang at my place

She did not reply. A photo came in from Allan shortly after, a sunset in New Mexico. *You'd like it here... how's that breaststroke*

She paused on the image, a russet plateau under clouds that looked scant and uneven, like what a child has left on a plate. Then she turned off her phone. Still in her bathing suit she passed inside and began on a fire in the woodstove, her knees coming pale through the holes in her jeans. On the side of the refrigerator, visible from where she sat, was a snapshot of Allan at thirty, handsome in a black V-neck and holding a baby face-out. He looked nothing like her father, a boomer ruined by cigarettes and political paranoia, an embittered person who honked through her school parking lots in large, unreliable cars. Dead the August she was seventeen, he had been the sort who kept his hand on her neck in public, woke her up with bouquets on Valentine's and gave her all his little money. Nothing beyond that, not what you're thinking, at least not that we know of—but she started mentioning it with a kind of rage during one-on-one coffees, stomping up the sixty steps of that monument in the park toward the big Doric column. That's what passed for paternity, she said. Making your daughter your little wife. He was a cashier at a convenience store, and there were years he could not afford two bedrooms. On the mattress next to him, she had no choice but to feel him twitch as he slept. She hated it, and spent her childhood in classrooms and libraries, or going between the two. This she confessed to one of us who was, at least politically, at least online, interested in matters of class.

To the group Helen never spoke of money, and neither, obviously, did we. It was easy to forget. She had convinced us a long time before that she belonged, if she had not convinced herself.

————

Where was her mind? Well, to be fair, she swam elsewhere the next day—drove the thirty minutes to the ocean and let it abuse her, saying in an obnoxious post that what she liked about it was how it made a fool of everybody, eventually. But she stopped at the ice-cream place right near the river, Big Daddy's, staffed entirely by boys of that age, mossy-breathed creatures waiting to be let into the next part of their lives. It was not a surprise that he pulled up right in front of the wood picnic table she sat atop, her knees wide apart and her hair attenuated with salt. He didn't look at Helen as he approached the empty sales window, which he slid himself onto and leaned way through, calling out the name of the friend somewhere inside. When no one answered he sidled over and stood in her sun.

The water nymph is ice-cold, he said. Kinda predictable. Then he reached for a strand of her hair and tugged.

That did it. He texted her the address while she could still see him, from the driver's seat of his car, a red Volvo station wagon with taupe leather interior. At his age Helen Tiel had passed for older, something in how languidly she could sit on a barstool, or how loosely she tied the sashes of trench coats, as though the mood of the evening might change with a hook of her finger, from outdoor to in, public to private, clothed to not. Prom was mostly a bar in San Francisco where something with a mustache pawed her lower back, college the law student with big bleached teeth whose notes on torts she read aloud in his bed.

His parents' house was full of Peaks Island ceramics, imperfect textiles hung and draped, Shaker chairs positioned near moody charcoals. A basset hound passed with ancient regret through the neat, cool rooms. It was a house whose imperfections were celebrated, the warped quality of the fanlights telling the age of the glass. He brought her on a tour with a finger in her belt loop—she showed up in jeans, a leather jacket with an oversized sheepskin collar, not the watch she loved, men's, twenties, which she mentioned to us once she kept on during sex, a way of making the act more a part of the measured world. The appeal and offense of her was that privacy did not really register. That boy had a young face that predicted the older: a smirker, not a winker, who would get lines around his mouth before marks around his eyes. This is me, he said, pushing open a door and releasing a smell that was secret and total. The bed was tightly made, the skateboards lined up precisely along the baseboard. She made it through two offers of a drink before she relented.

Then he led her outside, through a garden of hyacinth and milkweed, toward a Ping-Pong table set up in high grass. She learned the names of the others, a shallow nodding blur of Theo and Matt and Forrest, and slipped off her sneakers. Barefooted she leapt easily, with her painter's wrists she played well, and a few matches later she was joining into their cries. They swore at vindictive overhand slams, they marveled at short-stopping spins. Back in the house when a pizza arrived, Helen was quiet again, trying to believe she had come with a benign curiosity about them: boys, whose affection she hadn't considered viable when she was their age, opting for the more practiced lines of men. If the accessories had changed, the real cigarettes gone, the phones you flipped open to press physical buttons, the noises had not, the posture. That teenage male tendency, when passing under an open doorway, to jump up and tap the lintel.

If she had stepped down the hall then, if she had called us to confess—well, she wouldn't have called us, it's true we had made our boundaries clear. What Helen wanted from friendship was the sort of girlhood intimacy that smeared. Hands held like lovers, all depths revealed, no question too personal, no obligation on the horizon. If her watch was beautiful, she hated when you looked at yours. Watching the debates at Allison Feineman's, the night Trump stalked Hillary like a finger-puppet shadow, Helen simply got up and fell asleep in the guest bedroom. *Would you mind* are three words she had never used. Although this leaves out something we shouldn't forget— when it came to us, when it came to something we needed, she usually didn't mind. Helen loved to be turned to, she was a fetcher of prescriptions, would troll the internet for furniture on your behalf. When the shyest of us admitted to her brother's diagnosis of schizophrenia, Helen had a sense of the right questions to ask, as she often did about places that were tender. Coming from a life where they did not apply, she knew where idioms would pale.

By and large, we had stopped inquiring about her love life, if it could be called that. Some of us felt taunted by these details, her high-budget sexual expenditures. The months before the most traditional of us married, confessing to Helen she felt afraid of monogamy—there had only been a boy at Dalton, a boyfriend at Yale, then Ben—Helen said this fear was normal. Then she began to chat, with too little transition, about the surfer who made her orgasm near a cliff on a hike, the war photographer who tied her to his iron desk. As the worst men do, she took pride in her conquests, saw them as a picture book she could turn for the story of the world that wanted her. Maybe a hundred in her lifetime, though we didn't ask, knowing she would have made a fool of us somehow. You can't say whore and we would never say whore—well, once we said whore—but you could say without qualms there was trouble.

———————

He took her hand then and led her from the kitchen onto a deck—he pointed out the moon and surprised her with a kiss. Did he ask then, did he ask almost anything about her, and shouldn't she have known what it meant if he didn't? If it was the other way, if he had really believed her to be a girl alone, shouldn't he have felt suspicious of the kind of responses she gave, her lack of slang, her studied comportment? Helen had energy, yes, a feeling for spontaneity, but she sat as an adult sits. Her adjectives were a woman's. He mentioned majors, being torn between two parts of himself, the one that made and the other that thought. Alternating between sips of nicotine and weed, he told her about his childish idea, a water bottle that filtered for certain bacteria. She patronized him vaguely, suggesting that, if he wanted to assist countries left behind by globalization, he probably should learn more about the market forces that had kept them back. Smart and beautiful, he said. What can't she do? He pulled a flask from his back pocket and held it starward and she nodded. When they had each taken a long drink he put an arm around her shoulder and asked if he could trust her with a secret. I've been choking my dog, he said—at first only if she barked as I came in late, but then I started to wonder if she even remembered, so I started doing it mornings before track. Helen had nothing to say to this confession, and the boy may have sensed he had gone too far. Holding a few fingers around her pinkie, he brought her back to his room.

The clues to what he had been, a flexion of boyhood ago, hung from the pegs of his walk-in closet, under track team sweatshirts the recital medals, behind folded sweaters the stickers pressed on wood. His hand shot up inside her before she'd set down her drink. He pulled down her pants and kissed her there lightly, a few times. There was no performance. The silence of it was astonishing, a reminder of what sex was before it annealed with life. When it seemed still like another country, when it could be felt as only luck. "Old could be fun," she thought she heard one of his friends say, as they fell to the bed, a shadow pausing by the door, but the boy acted like he hadn't heard. Her age, she might have realized then, had never belonged to her: she'd been younger or older, the thing by which somebody else felt a sense of himself. He and Helen were in there a long time, the party on the other side of the door changing. Twenty boys more arrived, thirty. A small fire in the kitchen sink, a stairway with a plush runner they raced down on cardboard pulled from the recycling.

———

Did she do it because she believed she had fooled him, or because she wanted to know her age was irrelevant? The spring before this, in a white hooded scarf loosely wound, Helen told us she felt relieved of who she was in the sex she had: not in terms of personal freedom, exactly, but in the similar way all those men looked behind her. Though seduction might be tailored to the man, during the act itself she experienced a kind of spiritual multiplication—she was every person that man had ever slept with, roughly the same arc of sensations, and he was every man who had ever been rough or supplicant with her. She felt more a part of the world, fucking and being fucked, knowing the same gestures had been repeated by someone else alive. Maybe we nodded when she said so, passed the shared dessert. What could we say to that but: Check please? What could we think but: Be careful?

It was her upbringing that was responsible, some of us thought. How life with her creep of a father left her solitary, a walker, making up halves of telephone conversations she believed she'd someday have. She said more than once that this might have been what was really wrong, that in having no family she was without some crucial record, without the ability to see her life as something responsible to itself. Helen missed California, but would never go back. The fall of the separation, one of us with a big Catholic family brought her to Philadelphia for Thanksgiving. Helen was patient through the tour of the renovations, faintly wicked when she saw the childhood oil portraits. Charming through turkey, stoic come a long vacation anecdote that occurred over pie. Strolling the suburb after, kissing our friend's face and pointing out peculiarities in architecture, Helen said that such a clean division of before and after—the cheap shirts and big tantrums of her father, the city across the country that reshaped her—made her think the latter was something she had dreamed. Our Catholic friend stopped to admonish Helen. That's not how dreaming works, she said, or something like it. When you wake up, it's the before that wasn't real.

Maybe my understanding is confused, Helen snapped. You know I've always had trouble sleeping.

If that was not a strong point, it was a part of the truth. Her mother was gone by five, but even before, when she was very young, when she was very blond, when she struggled with then conquered the sound of the *w*, Helen Tiel had the insomnia of some middle-aged widow. She haunted the house that her sleeping parents rented, playing a game she called only Emergency. Wearing a T-shirt of her father's, her bare bottom touching the warped wood floor where she crouched, she arranged plastic cars and disproportionate dolls, whispering as she condemned their situation with crises of health and time. There were hospitals, in that hallway, that would never be reached, crashes that could not be avoided. Roads often gave onto gorges, was the point of the game, good lives turned bad all at once.

———

She never asked his age, as certain men above her had once not asked hers. Just before midnight his parents returned home, asking those boys—as they found them hidden in the shower and pantry, the sunroom and linen closet—to call for mothers and fathers. Their rage about the bottles retrieved from the cellar, the water marks on the wood, was gelid: there was no warning, not even a knock, when they opened the door on their child and Helen. Get dressed, they said, right now.

Minutes later, looking from their son on the couch to the woman standing in the glut of lights they'd turned on, his parents were solemn and brief. Helen treaded time there, trying to find her jacket on the crowded rack. Hanging over her shirt was a gift from her husband, a simple gold necklace in the shape of branches. The boy, his posture humped and feet enormous, slurped as he cried, pulling at the string of his hooded sweatshirt so his face became smaller. His parents mentioned the carpet, they mentioned the wine. Two thousand dollars at least, they said, a figure that changed his features again but which did nothing to shock Helen. It was around then they really saw her. The boy saw what blew between his parents then, a question that they put first to him. How old is she? I don't fucking know, he said, defensive until he saw that a certain answer, a certain number pertaining to Helen, would soften them. Then they turned to her. I am very sorry, Helen said, her jacket on now, reaching for the door. She must have kept her eyes on the odometer as she ten-and-two'd the ten miles back, and that they didn't follow her must have seemed like a last stroke of luck. Her shoes she abandoned to the mist of the garden, left as she'd shed them to win her quick game.

How drunk had she needed to be to go into his room, how drunk was she still when she drove? She made it most of the way safely, and then she stopped at the river, swimming across naked, a faint interruption in the plane of black. But back in the car, at the edge of Allan's property where she paused to back up, seeing a car speeding toward her and not trusting it would stop, she reversed too quickly. It was just like Helen to do the damage herself. The accident was minor—a taillight, a fender, the pole in Allan's driveway—but because all the mechanics in town knew Allan she had to tell him, early the next morning, in a text that he replied to with a phone call she ignored. She thought some packing tape could cover the crushed white plastic for now, and stepped into his cluttered office, a place of few right angles and dented file cabinets, the desk and stacks of paper on it bloated from the salt of the fog. Opening a drawer where he'd told her once to look for a hammer, moving aside a shoebox, she found a photograph of his bottom half. A woman's hand on his cock and right under it his, the same turquoise ring on his middle finger.

Oh no!!! It's just a car, he wrote, a little later. *But send a photo of you to let me know you're OK.*

———

New York gives off a sense of the people who've left it—decent furniture left out, handbags strung from iron posts—and on trains there's the difference between those who have found some peace, standing calm in the trembling minutes over the bridge, and those who huff their way to a place by the window. To think about where Helen might be, there's a game we sometimes play, Dom in Detroit, Buddhist in Boise, Manacled in Monaco. As for what happened in Maine, Helen told only the quietest of us, knowing she wouldn't be interrupted, only the outline of facts. She deleted her accounts in the week that followed. The last texts anyone sent went through as delivered, and in reply to emails came a vague out-of-office with no stated terminus. It was, what—*I am deeply unavailable, and I wish you the best.*

Together we agreed it was inevitable, what became of Helen. Her life had begun to seem like some thing a child has built all day, the materials incommensurate with the bigness of the plans. For the child, there is a bitter relief in felling that flimsy thing, and going early to bed. We were included in a certain vision of hers, and then she put that vision down.

Though there is something easy to infer about shame, isn't there also the chance she had finally come to the thing she was after? To belong to no one, to be nowhere anyone could say. With each other, some of us called her a criminal or something like it, but in the privacy of our thinking, we only called her a woman, one who had been, too recently and with too much encouragement, a girl. We know we are lucky not to feel the uncertainty she did. In our homes, with our husbands, there is never really the question of what to do. As an adult, you build your life so that it goes on without your interruption, what is required purchased ahead of time and what is known about your marriage generally what has always been. Trying to comfort her, we said as much to Helen, how all that changes are your mornings, the dark things we can't help but sometimes think when dragged from sleep. If you wake up unhappy, you find the plans made, in the absence of your sorrow, a consolation. That's terrible, she said, she wanted nothing predicted for her. Helen wanted the episodic existence of a man, the new eras of the self encouraged and forgiven—deviations and catastrophes ultimately understood, in her mind as well as others', not as distress, but as courage.

There are moments, alone, when we think we understand it. Finding the wool trousers from grad school with the theater tickets in the pockets, slipping down the hall with the vibrator to the half bath and never crying out. Feeling not enough at the Montessori stations of zippers and toy boats, turning at night from our husbands' fat backs. We think we have solved it, the mystery of Helen, whether she was swimming at night because she wanted to live or because she hoped to die. In the water all superfluous movement is revealed, the gestures of the calf or forearm that bring nothing further. She was asking, as she fought the current, if her body was necessary. She was finding it was not. And this was good news, for a time, as she waited to discover some aspect of her that would be.

That her life fell away from ours was nothing we could help. But if you had trusted her with the story of what some man did to you—in a room, after all, you'd agreed to enter, in a position you did not stop him from bending you into, with his fingers in your mouth, which you could have bitten—and felt her hand come straight for yours under the table: you would, we think, have liked her. The teeth marks on her passport, the avoidable disasters. How she glowed down Carlton at the end of her jog, yelling your name across traffic. Anybody's suffering might amount to how often they have to look over their shoulder, hoping not to be followed by someone they were, or someone they feared, at the beginning. As a baby, Helen must have been like any other, curious about what her father handed her, immaculate of the rest.

WORSHIP

♦

Half his boxes were already unloaded in their new apartment when she learned about the woman who'd called the police on him. They'd been in Nashville two days. The night before, he'd insisted on a campy welcome—honky-tonk night at the American Legion down Gallatin Pike—and they had popped the brass hook right off the inside of a bathroom stall. She had heard its clatter and expected him to stop, but he just moved them to the adjacent wall. Sex in the bathroom was a first for Hannah, one of many in a season with Phillip. He once washed her feet, came to her where she lay on the couch with a deep pot of suds, and gestured with a twist of his index finger that she sit up. Besides her, he loved mornings, the rosemary in his backyard, a beagle he'd had ten years, and Willie Nelson. Phillip was the last of three sons, and the only one to leave west Texas.

They spent the next morning packing up his one-bedroom, a little hungover, calling out the refrains of overdone ballads they'd heard the night before as they misremembered them. The Clock Loves Me Better Than You. Even the Dog Knows You're with Somebody Else. Early afternoon they stopped by a

market for to-go lunch and drove down to the Parthenon, set-
tling on a concrete bench by the man-made lake that faced it.
He pulled a baseball from his windbreaker, threw the jacket
aside, and began a jokey game for her amusement, tossing it in
the air with his hand and rebuffing it with the perfect curve of
his bicep. She watched this laughing as she ate salad from an
à la carte box, covering her mouth. The dog watched too, with
patient interest, raising his gray eyebrows. Phillip looked, at
thirty-four, like someone who could ruin a marriage in under a
week—always a toothpick coming from the side of his mouth,
a hank of dark hair fallen onto his forehead, a hip bone shot
slightly forward. Wherever they went, women bent toward him
like reeds under hands. It was early December, and sunshine
smelled like nothing when it was cold.

A tattoo on his left forearm, the dark line of a circle, was
a reference to an ex, Hannah knew. Though there was nothing about Hannah he did not want to know, the seventh-grade
drama teacher who'd kissed her in the red velvet curtains, the
suicides shot through both sides of her family like a warning,
her feeling about his past was not entirely the same. When
it came to certain misfortunes, she thought a general outline
would have done as well. As a teenager, he'd fallen to shoplift-
ing, school supplies and groceries, and paid with a month in
a juvenile detention facility. In his mid-twenties, a back injury
on a warehouse job left him with an opiate addiction—he'd
overcome it without rehab, took no small pride in that. His
mother had beaten him, hangers in the shower. They had said
I love you quickly, as if there might not be time later.

After warming up with slapstick grunts and grins, he took to the game he'd designed for himself with real solemnity, adding challenges, canting his trunk to bounce the ball from the tricep every other throw. The tattoo surfaced and turned, and behind him the replica of antiquity stood, slightly off, the warmth of the color too well distributed. In the evenings they slept entwined, his resting temperature always higher than seemed normal, and sometimes he lay her flat on his chest, like a baby. He could sleep like that, her whole life on top of him, could sleep anywhere. Coming upon her that morning where she stood assembling the last cardboard boxes, he'd taken her from behind and laughed, pointing. On some the flaps were locked against each other one way, on some another, the pattern of tape varying a little. "What are these," he had said, "Impressionist boxes? I love whatever dream you were in." When he was jocose he was goading, repeating the punch line from the room he passed into, or as the waiter came by, or when the traffic died down and the car was quiet. Hannah knew she would hear it again, sometime that day, a surprise rejoinder coming from the recesses of his thinking. Impressionist boxes! But in tenderness he was spectacular, adept with her anxiety, pressing a hand to her chest and reminding her of simple things that would always be true—the gifts she had, her general health—and he photographed her often, her lips open as she read, an ankle draped over the lip of the tub. "Jesus," he had said once, a month in, stopping in the street, interrupting something she was saying about her work. "I just got a flash of you pregnant in the bath." She worried about aging, and his love of her future seemed to absolve her of that concern. Four months, they'd been together. In bed he was rough, something she hoped she wanted.

————————

On the drive down to Nashville—he had picked her up in New York, insisting when she called it impractical that he wanted to bring her home personally—they had chatted garrulously, the conversation switching topics with every turn in light or scenery. When their talk finally settled, she felt her feet press at the rubber mat. It was a class issue, he said, violence.

"That's something you have to understand if we're going to be together."

"But we are together," she had interjected. "We are currently en route to a very real apartment we've rented to live in." Her fingers curled around the vinyl door handle, she listened, though the premise to her was suspect: she had not grown up wealthy, in any sense of the word, and what he sometimes suggested was her elevated status seemed more to do with preferences she had for quiet, or privacy, or order. Jackie O, he called her, when she asked about the wine list at a restaurant, or for twenty more minutes to read before they left the house. In bed once, he had imitated the triangle she made of her napkin, holding a corner of sheet up to his pursed mouth and saying, "But waiter, is the wine made by *priests* or *monks*?" She laughed as she swatted him: he could delight her, he could make her a child.

He had gone on and on, the flat of his right hand taut against the wheel as he explained. In Texas, in a town drilled to death and sinking into the fields that had been its only promise, he and his brothers had learned to fight as a necessity. Of course he didn't enjoy it, he told her, of course there was not joy in the sight of blood on asphalt. But they had been bullied: because of what their house looked like, because if they brought lunches to school it was in the branded plastic bags of the grocery outlet where their mother shopped drunk. Boys richer than him, in clothes cleaner, had followed him back to his house, patient with the turns he might take to put off the destination. Though they might push and slap, when he learned to fight he found he was better at it, for hurting someone meant debasing yourself, too, and that was something they'd been taught, by the safety of their houses and the love of their families, was wrong. "I got him in the teeth, then I kneeled over him and brought his chin down on a driveway, opened it up," he said, about a bully named William. "I was scraped up and freaked out, but after that he respected me. Used my name when he saw me in the halls." Hearing him speak this way, Hannah felt both violated and censored—it was not fair that he give her that picture, but it was also not her place to draw the connection between the son who was beaten and the boy who could fight.

"Stop at the next gas station," she'd said, not qualifying it. Walking around side to where the dumpsters kissed the restroom doors, she called her closest girlfriend, saying she needed to confess something directly and quickly. Somewhere in Los Angeles, chopping vegetables on speaker,

calling out occasionally to her toddler, Michelle was reasonable and helpful, describing how she'd felt upon learning her
husband had been, a few times in college, the instigator of
some bar fight.

"It was horrific to imagine," she said, "but after a few
months I saw those stories, basically, as a few data points
receding, rather than anything prefiguring our life together, or
his treatment of me. Some of it has to be the horror of growing
up in a male body in this country, doesn't it?" Michelle said.
"He's never hurt you, has he? You've never felt afraid he would
hurt you?" From where she paced, Hannah could see Phillip,
his hands behind his head where he stood by the car, and he
turned just then and waved, nervously, seeing the phone in her
hand. He hadn't broken eye contact when she stepped out of
his sight line again.

"No," Hannah said, stopping in her mind on the faces he
made in bed, then thinking that unfair. "And you're right—as
a girl you don't even consider it an option, but as a little boy
aren't you basically obligated to pretend at war?" Though Hannah had felt ashamed of her rapid intimacy with Phillip—his
visits to New York, during which she did little and saw next to
no one; the promises and platitudes; the relocation, the sign-
ing of the lease—Michelle had been supportive: they were rare,
they told each other, women who followed their real wishes
easily. Besides, on a weekend Phillip and Michelle were both
visiting New York, he had cooked the three of them dinner,
and had impressed Michelle. Hannah had shown her a book
of his photos, just released and critically welcomed, but Phillip

had spoken mostly about volunteering as an escort at an abortion clinic. He talked often and in broad terms about his country, expressing disdain for the coastal cities. I'm just a redneck, he would say, laughing, looking around the room as if to check, but New York's not the only place.

In the parking lot in front of her, an old condom caught the light, unwrapped but unused, and the sounds of the gas station came in bursts when the automatic door opened, an argument about a lottery ticket, a song that listed cities and states like blessings. Thinking of Michelle's face, the way it cycled through feeling on behalf of those she cared for, Hannah said goodbye, and I love you, and returned to the car. Though her heart rate had normalized, she was exhausted, and when Phillip asked about her call, she answered only the name of her friend. After fifty miles of silence he apologized, close to tears. "I shouldn't have scared you like that," he said, taking her hand across the gearshift. "I was trying to tell you about how it was, but it must have seemed like how it is." She had squeezed his hand in return, expecting faith to rush in.

When they pulled up to their new home she waited for the hope she'd felt, as he had video-guided her through it three weeks before, at the built-in postwar shelving, at the large dining room for which he said he'd build a table, at the idea of an affordable city where people said good morning. She was going to be in love, she was going to be as quiet as she often felt. Though her things were being shipped from New York, and none of his had been unpacked, they stayed there, that night, unrolled the brand-new mattress onto the floor. She had a hard time sleeping, and tried to focus on the ease of his breathing next to her. Sometime near one a.m. he called out, in real joy, "Oh! Beautiful!"—as if he'd been surprised by a color he'd never seen before—and she laughed, as if she could see it. Hannah and Michelle had spoken once of a certain banal dream, in which you discover another room in the place you've been living a long time. It was the summer they were twenty-eight, both about to leave men who had made them unhappy, Michelle for a director across the country. Laughing over coffee, kicking at leaves in Brooklyn, they'd talked about what a female fantasy this was, how neither knew a man who'd had it. But when Hannah had met Phillip two years later, over drinks after his opening, he'd described this dream to her exactly—the relief at finding that door, the foolishness of believing, bitterly, that life was limited. She'd thought then, as she did again, her hand on his sleeping chest, that if the suffering he recounted made her uncomfortable, it also made him someone who might love her better, and someone more worthy of her love. He had woken her with donuts the next morning, already having jogged happily through the morning, and orange juice he tipped to her mouth in bed.

————

Feeling the dare of the weather, the thrill of their lives coming closer together, she watched the ball float toward sun and return to shadow, and she asked about the permanent circle. She knew only the girlfriend in question had been a teacher of some kind, that she had helped him crawl out of the hole his injury had made of his life.

"Who was she?" she said, pointing. "How did it end?"

When the ball fell past his elbow he curled his fingers but lost it, narrowly, and it rolled down the slope toward the bench where she sat. Sitting down next to her, he didn't bother at all with its retrieval, and it skulked near them like something another person had forgotten. When his dog approached, Phillip took him in his lap. "It ended very badly," he said. "It was very unhealthy. Do you really want to know?" He looked at her with the face of someone woken in the middle of the night, the alarm of holding two worlds.

That he asked this question in a voice of blame confused her: as though she would be the one held accountable to what had happened in his past. But she also sensed some hypocrisy he might impute to her if she said she did not, after all, want to know—he would accuse her, as he had tacitly in the car, of wanting to love only parts of him. "Of course I want to know," she said. "It's your life." As did the most dangerous lies, it felt right, even freeing, to tell.

He began with details she already knew, bringing in the shape of a woman among them. The forklift he drove through the warehouse, the heavy pallets of weed that occasionally had to be hoisted by hand, the sudden pain that became chronic, the purple days in bed, the black future. The oxy. She was a natural caretaker, he said, and somehow fell for him then: all the way down to where he was, his spiritual nadir. In the daytimes she substituted for kindergartens in beautiful sixties housedresses, yellows and reds, and in the evenings it was movies in bed, Antonioni, Capra, the tiny feathers from the down comforter falling up, the splashless vanishing of a woman off a sailboat, the shimmering eyes of Claudette Colbert.

"Weird to think: shimmering because of the silver nitrate in the film then." He paused. "So flammable it could burn underwater."

"I know that," Hannah snapped. "Go on." Her arms around herself, she turned her face from the false ruin to the man-made lake. She hated models of things, she remembered, whatever was excluded in the imitation of a shape, or an essence.

"It became a problem for her when I started to recover—when my life was mine again. Even though she had helped me, cutting pills in half, bringing me suboxone, by the time I was a month clean, two, she hated it. That I wasn't always home when she got there. That I was making my own dinner. You can't imagine what it's like to feel like your body is subjugated by something that wants to kill you."

"I'm a woman. I think I might. You were living together? How soon?"

"Almost immediately. Her place."

"So what happened?"

"There was a night I came home late. I'd been with friends, guys I hadn't seen in six months. Hadn't called, had been drinking, which worried her. Second I got in the door, lots of questions. I was on the defensive. I told her I needed some quiet. She shoved me. *She* shoved *me*."

Passing by them were college students, new parents, aging people alone in the kind of pants that had been fashionable when they were young. Hannah was almost angry with them, envious of how they would observe her and Phillip, an attractive couple sitting close together. He twisted the heel of his hand into his eye socket, and when he removed it, turned his face to the ground. It was as if the baseball there occurred to him for the first time, and he picked it up, running a thumb along the red lines that held it together. Please don't throw that ball, she felt herself begging in her mind. He did not. That the silence between them was frightened on either side filled her with a flashing resentment: that at this moment she had to feel his fear of her.

Hannah asked Phillip then why his girlfriend had shoved him, though she was not invested in the question because she suspected the answer would not be true. He was saying something about how she had wanted him to leave, but he had needed to get into the bathroom, take his allergy medication, and was only trying to get it, was of course going to heed her wish, though all he wanted was to talk it through, and it made no sense that she reached for the phone, and he was trying to tell her she didn't need protection, that he was her protection, that the police had no place in their life, but she was beyond reaching and that was how it happened: he was crouching over her, holding the vase that had appeared to him, close by on the mantel. "She was acting like I was a total stranger, like we hadn't built anything. She wouldn't say anything but 'leave.' She shoved me when I tried to get into our room."

In response to the gesture Hannah made, an arc of her hand urging he tell her the worst truth, he answered. "Just once." His hands stayed over his face, though when he removed them, after a minute, she noticed he had not been crying.

"Where?" she said.

"Left temple."

"Did it ever happen again," Hannah asked. "Her or anyone."

"No," he said, each hand splayed before him now, as if pushing at a stuck door.

She asked to leave then. She said she needed to lie down. She was speaking quickly, hearing the blood in her head as she did during the worst of her anxiety—it felt as if the world in public might fold into accordion creases, flattening her with it. When they reached the house, when they stood in the door-frame of the bedroom they'd filled with his boxes, he moved to the bed on the floor and began making it, tightly, push-ing cardboard out of the way to clear a margin around it. The sheets were new and the corners tugged tight—he was pre-cise in all things, a person of immaculate fingernails and per-fect acceleration—but when she got in that bed, what Hannah thought was that her whole life had been stained, that each decision she'd made had led her here, and so each had been wrong, and so each had been filthy. I'm too fucked up, he was saying, I have to get out of here, calling to the dog to follow him. Hannah chose sleep then, stepped into the place under her thoughts and slammed the door.

When she came to, the winter dark was lilac through the glass, and inside the smell of cheap white paint more apparent.

The facts came with the parts of her body she moved to awaken them. With the curl of her right foot: he'd hit a woman. With the rotation of her neck: he'd never hit her. Twist of spine—she'd moved to Nashville. Roll of her shoulders—had taken his certainty for her own. Hinge of jaw—he'd been hit as a kid. Flex of fingers, held her all night. Tongue against teeth, tried to fuck her face.

Hannah moved the comforter aside, trying to chill herself awake, and blinked into the rims of his boxes, a haphazard few he'd left unsealed. She saw the brass pot of his grandmother's, which he revered and polished. A book of poems he loved, a copy of which he'd sent her in the mail—lavender pressed inside, ink on the title page, the word *happy* scrawled in a rush in his inconsistent hand. He'd written her name followed by an exclamation mark, like she was a curse word to be shouted at life's indifference. Though he was careful in his rituals she saw now he'd been wild in his packing, pillows with cords, knives wrapped in scarves. She reached for her phone and walked to the front door and stepped onto the veranda, where through the mesh were trees she didn't know the names of, cars throwing outsized shadows down the silent street.

Michelle picked up on the first ring, greeting Hannah, as she always did, as if they had just met by chance in some patch of sun. "Hey!" When they were together people took them for lovers, the way each mistook the other's body for her own, Michelle wiping crumbs from Hannah's mouth, Hannah passing a hand into the nest of Michelle's hair. In photos they looked like little girls, midway through some joke

that excluded any other question. Michelle had encouraged
Hannah when she started translating, at twenty-five. It was
a career whose call she had feared for its little money and
deep quiet, but Michelle, taking her shoulder in a crosswalk
and nearly barking, set her straight: "I can tell by how you
speak of this it's how you're meant to be alive," she said. Hannah had quit her bad office job that week, taken on her first
book-length assignment that month. They had celebrated on
Michelle's American Express, having too many in a restaurant
where they didn't yet belong, but the waiter had loved them
and brought a round on the house, delighted by the look on
their faces that said: Did you know? Did you know I love my
spectacular friend?

"Tell me what it is," Michelle said now, hearing the way
Hannah said her name, the only word she could think of.
Together they reviewed the facts. Hannah mirrored Phillip's
emphasis, that *she* had shoved *him*. She was not quite able to
say the things she feared most, though she knew they would
likely change Michelle's answer: what Phillip wanted from her,
sometimes, when they were naked. The clarity in his face, the
laugh, when he described childhood revenge.

"If his mother beat him, if his mother really beat him, if
that is what women were to him first, if she was the love in his
life but also the violence—"

"Yes," Hannah said, with a quiet enthusiasm, urging the
logic Michelle might find in a situation that left her insensate.

"Is it possible that was psychically significant, this thing
that happened with that woman? That he needed to feel what

it was to push back, which he never did with his mother, and also that it did nothing for him, that it felt wrong and went nowhere?"

Hannah, nodding on the porch, passed a hand over her face. She was awake now, and they talked the red flag down to a yellow, the danger from its attachment to her. Would a woman, they asked each other, who had shoved back: Would she have been thought of the same way? Would you judge me if I'd done it? No, they said. No. As she always did, Michelle returned Hannah to peace, like someone who finds something that has been removed from where it belongs, and restores it tenderly to its place on the shelf.

When Phillip came home, an hour later, he roasted vegetables in silence, basted tofu with sesame, and didn't turn when she came into the kitchen, thanking him for the plates he'd just set down on milk crates. He'd brought the dog to a friend's for the night, he mentioned, thinking it would be easier on him. Their fighting was making the dog anxious. Hannah cradled Phillip from behind as he salted the skillet, and waited for a response, which he refused her for a cool minute—but then he turned and lifted her, one hand under her legs and the other up her shirt. Leaving the dinner uneaten, he carried her to the bedroom, where they never turned on a light but his eyes gave off plenty, and he did something he had the first night they were together: a moment before he moved inside her, he took an amethyst ring he wore on his hand and slipped it onto hers. She laughed, as she had then, in astonishment. He worshipped her, she knew that.

————

In the morning they drove to the cemetery for a run, and when she stepped out of the car and moved to put her headphones in he stopped her. "It's better if you can hear your breathing," he said. "Also, I'd miss you." This bothered her—she never ran without music, which tricked her into motion—but he bent and kissed her and she assented. As they padded across brown grass and twisting gravel, she watched the perfect alignment of his hips with his shoulders, how he stopped sometimes to jog backward, waving at her mid-twirl with a playful flourish of the pinkie. It was cold enough, low forties, that keeping her heart rate up felt like a necessity, but twice he stopped, at a gravestone he wanted her to see, and commented at length on her form. "You lift your knees so high," he said. "I think it's energy you don't need to spend. I think it slows you down some." Hannah nodded, wishing they were running somewhere with fewer shadows, or with any flowers not left there for the dead.

They had lunch after at a meat-and-three, collard greens and okra and cornbread. Though Hannah barely spoke he smiled at her as though she were speaking, as though she were giving voice to a profound idea. As they passed out of the restaurant, the string of bells going off behind them, a man approached asking for change, and Phillip pulled the bills he had from his jogging-shorts pocket, then gestured for Hannah to hand the man their leftovers, which she did. Phillip put a hand on his shoulder, telling him what the box contained, then asked where he was sleeping that night. Pulling his denim jacket closer, the man pushed his gray tongue against his brown teeth as he enumerated possibilities of shelter. As the list went on, Hannah felt a muted surprise, for it seemed, though none of the choices were ideal, that there was no lack of bad options. The car ride home was quiet, save a honk Phillip gave at a Mercedes that cut him off.

Phillip left her there to make a last run to his old place, saying he looked forward to mopping, the pine scent, and asking that she keep an eye out for a certain tapestry, a relic of his uncle's, which he wanted to hang right away. She unpacked badly through the afternoon, finding half an hour had passed and she would only have moved a box from one room to another, surfacing from her thinking to find a single object in her hand. A jump rope of his, a seventies amber paperweight. If the boxes were hers, would she have left him alone with them? She knew the answer was no, that she would have been embarrassed to leave him to her disorder, would have insisted he only handle things they'd bought together. In New York she'd put the clothes and objects she'd culled out on her stoop, then watched, through the window, as tall men with long faces fingered those parts of her life. When he had called to say he thought she should move to Tennessee, she evaluated the possibility as she did any other suggestion of travel, wondering about the grain something new would create against the darker parts of her. For three years she'd been living in a one-room apartment that faced the trash cans, doing her work at a nearby library, preparing the same salads, saving no money, feeling when the winter came that she might not live through it.

Just after sunset, Hannah sat with her spine against the bedroom baseboard, on her lap a shoebox of his photos labeled *San Francisco*. There were stacks of Polaroids, his life in the late aughts, groups of good-looking people in the Beatle boots and secretary blouses and Stetsons that were popular then, holding up beers where they sat on marble stoops. She thumbed through them with a real sweetness, seeing how he leaned with an electric guitar, how his hair had been long and he'd carried a leather bag on his shoulder. Under the Polaroids were a bundle of photo booth strips, rubber-banded, and in one of them a woman who shared the circle tattoo, the same place on the arm.

The particulars of the face came to Hannah like a list copied from a chalkboard, the most essential facts to be recalled once she was alone in her mind. A gap in the teeth that widened from the gum in a sixty degree angle. A mole at the left temple. Tawny hair in natural curls, styled halfway up. But the worst thing she saw—spread across four frames where they posed in surprise, anger, lunacy, and lust—was happiness. Put it away, Hannah heard Michelle advise her, and moments after Hannah had, there came the lights of his car, shining to her from where he'd just pulled into the driveway. The box went into the bedroom bureau, a piece they'd thrifted on her last visit and that he'd refurbished with new hardware, and she focused on the pile of his clothing he'd dropped in a laundry bag on the bed.

Phillip returned with a jaunty open mouth, removing the toothpick to wave it in emphasis as he told her about something

he'd seen on a walk down his old block, a meeting of two tod-
dlers on opposite sides of a chain-link fence. "He had these
little red corduroys on, and he kissed her right through the
diamond," he said, delighted, spreading his hands and making
a smacking sound with his mouth. "She didn't know what hit
her." In response to his story, she smiled a little and put a belt
of his away.

She felt quiet all evening, through dinner they cooked and
a drink they had on the couch, and Phillip asked, once with a
squeeze and once with a blunt gesture from where he sat opposite her, what was wrong.

"I think I need to take a bath," Hannah said, and she didn't
wait for his reaction, just passed into the little bathroom and
opened its one window. There was nothing she could use to
make any real bubbles, only his bar of almond soap, so she
ran the water plain and too hot, waiting on the toilet under
the little window. Her hand shot through to the winter air, she
turned a palm in the world outside. When the bath was ready
she got right in, gasping at the heat and kneeling to acclimate.
Phillip opened the door soon after, striding toward the window in his jacket and boots, asking if she wanted it closed and
bringing it shut. Then he settled narrowly on the rim of the
tub, his hands grasped between his knees. Again, he asked,
was she okay. Hannah calculated the cost—what it would take
not to mention the photo, not to mention the woman with the
circle on her body—and she knew the answer was another
night of sleep.

"You're thinking about her, aren't you?" he said, looking

at Hannah's face for confirmation and then cradling his own, hissing into his palms. "I fucking knew it, oh god, I fucking knew it." She understood already he was not talking to her, not really, and she took her knees against her chest, sitting up straight against the pink tile. "I knew this would happen," he was saying, to the thing inside him, and she waited, breathing evenly, for his return to the present, taking the knob of the faucet between two toes to bring some cold water. As he removed his fingers from where they pressed at his eyes, she was turning the knob back, and he watched that gesture with a pitiful shock: as though it were malicious of her, to make any changes to the world of her comfort, one he felt had excluded him.

"It's not going to work if you hold it against me," he said. "It's not going to work if you see it in everything I do. I more than paid for it then, Hannah. Please don't make me suffer for it now." I wish he would touch me, she heard herself think, then wondered why. Because she wanted to be paid that compassion. Because she did not want to pay it.

A silence passed, the steam dissipating, and she thought of the sort of talking that had raised her. Hannah's parents, when they were unhappy with her, had always asked for the story of the transgression. Tell us about how you made that decision, they would say, gentle at her bedside, beginning with how you felt in the time leading up to it. They had made it understood that they wanted to understand. Her parents had loved who she was as a child, had always asked what she'd dreamed.

"Just say something," he moaned.

"I'm sorry," Hannah said. "I found a picture of you two when I was unpacking. I knew it was her because I saw the tattoo."

Phillip shook his head and then stood up, leaning from where his heels pressed against the tub to the opposite wall—he gripped the mounted dowel. The points of his jaw stood out as he took the single towel from it and drew it to his cheeks, and Hannah heard herself apologize again.

"I'm sorry," she said. "It's just that I saw her face."

Her remark had the effect of an electrocution, briefly tightening everything about him before unfurling it. He whipped around, then crouched on the balls of his feet, rocking forward as he said what he did next.

"Did you think," he hissed, "she didn't have a face?"

He was out the door in a flat, black second. Hannah heard the front door slam and thought she saw a shock pass across the water. Seeing her body clearly where it was submerged, she stayed in the bath a long time.

When she finally got out, she took the towel he'd dropped from the tile and wrapped it around her, then moved into the dark clutter of the living room. At the same level as the boxes was a lamp on the floor, and she turned it on and sat by it, fingering the pink weft of the shade as she dialed Michelle on speaker. When the call stopped ringing, her friend's voice played into the room, happy and distracted, announcing her name and her promise to return the calls she hadn't answered. The texts from Phillip had already started coming in. This was a habit that had charmed her at first, how minutes after they separated, when a moment had passed, he felt the need to append language to it. *I loved how you stomped up those stairs,* he would write, or send a photo he'd taken of her right after they had sex, the secret smile on her face. He'd left his keys, she saw now, on a nail he'd driven into the plaster by the door. The detritus below remained, a patch of white dust.

You're my life and you give me life, he texted.

I am so lucky to be seen by you.

I am so sorry to have brought this bad weather into our home.

We will do whatever it takes to rebuild. We are not as small as our past but as big as our future.

I am out buying oils and bath salts and flowers. Sourdough. There is that nice white in the fridge and I want you to treat yourself to some.

Hannah.

Baby.

God I'm going to marry you someday

How you looked in the tub

I love your peace

In that room there was already the scent of him, neroli and loamy rolling tobacco, the sweat coming off his running shorts somewhere nearby, and though she doubted the room smelled of her, too, she knew this was part of being alive. Your sense of yourself was never quite accurate. You relied on others to mention who you were at the end, at the bottom, in the dark.

When a car passed, the curved iron grille on the front windows printed shapes on the hardwood, curves that looked like hooks. The patrol of shadows reminded Hannah she had lied about her doubts, wishing life would vanish them.

Crossing to the door, she moved the dead bolt, then the latch, to the right. If she took pride in her mind, she could not find the wisdom in the situation that surrounded her. Before him, there had been a string of men who had treated her well, but seemed held from imagination, emotional and otherwise, by a lifetime of luck. Sex had been something that happened, for a tolerable half an hour, after dinner. They'd been lawyers and journalists, good with silverware and birthday reservations, and their only crime had been their privilege, a native feeling that said disaster wasn't coming, and that their inner resources would be equal to any that might.

Though she spoke of it rarely, not wanting the losses to define her, there was no avoiding what it had done to her, losing both parents by the time she'd graduated college— a ceramicist and a carpenter, both lung cancer, a terrible coincidence, people said. Because who and what she'd come from were gone, she believed anything she had, or anything she was, would vanish with too abrasive a wind, that some crisis professional or logistical would totally undo her, send her back to grief permanently. But when the topic came up with the men she had chosen—for their neat apartments and sturdy demeanors, their healthy families and sweet nicknames—they had always seemed to reach for aphorism when what she needed was the complexity of myth, a story long enough to include sorrow with plenty else. PTSD, went the diagnoses from professionals, a summary that also seemed too brief. In the dark of the bedroom she crawled into the mess of sheets and comforters, and she fell asleep with her phone in her hand, the messages from him changing in pitch as they went unanswered.

Hannah

Baby

I'm on my way home

Are you ok?

Tell me

You can't ignore this at your convenience

We have to stay connected

She woke up to a gentle thumping, the rhythm and contact inconsistent. A loose drag of fingers, sometimes a slap. She listened to it in bed a minute, then rose to the door between the rooms with a sheet around her, pawing for the overhead switch. Against the white paint, the skin of the forearm as it came through the grille was voluminous, the only thing alive in the room, the clear center of energy. The veins on the arm seemed to feel the light, fill under it, the points of the fingers to pause in its attention. She thought she saw the keys, where they hung on the nail, tremble at the motion just beneath them.

"Hannah?"

He spoke the word with a peculiar hope—that somehow, it had been someone else who locked him out, and the answer to the question of her name would be no—and it was not dissimilar from hers: for an intruder who didn't know her, for a threat she hadn't loved, and chosen. The hand kept moving as he gently spoke, slapping near where the metal dangled. Can you let me in, he was saying. Do you see my keys there, I must have forgotten them. What are you doing, Hannah? What do you think we're doing?

"I'm sorry," Hannah said, to the amethyst ring, standing close enough now she could touch it. The color of it was as vivid as his voice was becoming.

"You fell asleep," he narrated. "I came home and the house was dark. I was trying to get back inside. I was just trying to get back to you, but now that you're up you can let me in." His fingers were still reaching. The dust displaced from the nail told her where the keys would land if they fell, an easy foot beneath the windowsill.

"Then why are you still moving your arm like that?" she asked. There was little feeling in her voice, just a curiosity, nearly scientific, as she saw the change in the form of her life—she'd be a woman who stayed with a violent man, or a woman so afraid of a man that she left him. She watched the arm retract. Then his face appeared in the window, sideways. He was bent on the porch on his hands and knees, and the T-shirt he'd left in, white and creaseless as he kept all of them, was marked now by bars of dirt from the grille.

"Is this better?"

He widened his eyes as she stepped back. Hannah, he was saying, I don't even have a jacket. She sat and crossed her legs, the sheet cresting her shoulders. It was true, it could not be ignored, that they had been raised very differently. He had never known a quiet house to be a comfort, only a threat of a loud noise to come. Gathering the sheet around her, Hannah went to the door and unlocked it.

————

Half an hour later, on a granite counter in Los Angeles, a phone lit up, a flashing thing among the bowl of lemons, the bouquet of car keys, and the child's purple drawing of a house. In the rooms above, the floors covered in maroon kilims, the beds in ironed linens, a woman lit incense and folded towels. On her finger was the ring her husband had given her, in the hall a framed photo of her and a friend at twenty-five.

The phone shook without pause for most of seven minutes, lighting up between calls to indicate new voicemails, then went silent and dark as the hills nearby. Outside, it was fire season. All along closed windows grew climbing jasmine, blossoms starved shut by smoke. The sky thrilled with an orange it would stay all night—odd, and real, and almost a comfort.

NATURAL LIGHT

◆

I won't tell you what my mother was doing in the photograph—or rather, what was being done to her—just that when I saw it for the first time, in the museum crowded with tourists, she'd been dead five years. It broke an explicit promise, the only one we keep with the deceased, which is that there will be no more contact, no new information. In fact, my mother, who was generally kind and reliable in the time she was living, had already broken this promise. Her two email accounts were frequently in touch. The comfort I took in seeing her name appear, anew in bold, almost outweighed the embarrassment of the messages that followed. She wanted me to know that a small penis size was not an indictment against my future happiness. She hoped I would reconsider a restaurant I might have believed to be out of my budget, given a deal it made her pleased to share. She needed some money for an emergency that had unfolded, totally beyond her control, somewhere at an airport in Nigeria. Though these transmissions alarmed me, it was nice to be able to say what I did, when an acquaintance or administrator at the college where I teach saw my eyes on my phone and asked, Something important? It was nice to

be able to say, Oh, it's just an email from my mother. Given
how frequently we had written while she lived—the minute
logistics of a renovation, my cheerful taxonomies of backyard
weeds—she avoided the spam filter after her death, and I could
not bring myself to flag her.

————————

She had not *died as she lived*. Does anyone? Though my mother
had not been vain in a daily sense, she often made me, in the
weeks of her dying, rub foundation onto the jaundice of her
skin. This was something she could have done alone—she
never lost power in her hands, as far as I knew—but one of
the dying's imperatives is to make the living see them. This
is nobody's fault, but it is everybody's burden. That sounds
like something my father would say, half-eating, in the general
direction of the television: Nobody's fault, everybody's burden.
Perhaps he did, and this thinking made its way into mine. I
don't always know well where I've left a window open.

The photo was part of a multi-artist retrospective, curated
less to discuss a school or approach than to cater to nostalgia
for a certain era in New York. Shows like these are a dime a
dozen here, and they are not of the sort I seek out, having lost
most interest I might have had in the type of lives and rooms
they always feature. Bare mattresses on the floor, curtains that
are not curtains, enormous telephones off the hook, the bodies
always thin but never healthy. Eyes shadowed in lilac, men in
nylon nighties pour liquor from brown paper bags into their
mouths. A woman with a black eye laughs, her splayed thigh

printed with menstrual blood. These photographs are in color, the light strictly natural. There is always some museumgoer finding her imprimatur there, looking affirmed and clarified about the ragged way she'd arrived feeling.

That day I had come to the museum for a show of paintings, landscapes of Maine refashioned with a particular pink glow the painter must have felt when he saw what inspired them. I was wearing a shirt that buttoned high on my neck, and my rose-gold watch, vintage, which I had just repaired. The wedding ring remained. It wasn't that I had any hopes for reconciliation, but its persistence on my finger was a way of matching inside to out. I needed to be reminded, when I caught myself deep in a years-old argument with my husband, alone and furious on the mostly empty midday subway, that he had been real—that my unhappiness was not only some chemical dysfunction of mine.

I decided to take the stairs, and then to pass through the exhibit in question: I had an hour to spare, and I thought it might be an interesting metric. How little I related could be the proof of a transformation I had undergone, a maturation evident in how I saw and felt. When my husband met me, twenty-two to his forty, he saw a girl with a rough kind of potential, and he tended to me as one might a garden, offering certain benefits and taking others away. He did not wish me to grow in just any direction. That I allowed him this speaks just as poorly of me. I was once a girl with an exquisite collection of impractical dresses—ruched chiffon, Mondrian prints—and a social smoking habit, a violent way with doors and windows.

I left him in taupes, my arches well supported, my thinking framed in apology. It is clear there were parts of me that must have been difficult to live with, namely an obsessive thought pattern concerning various ways I might bring about my own death, but also clear that I rose to the occasion of this malady with rosy dedication, running miles every day and recording the impact of this on my mind, conceiving of elaborate meals, the hedonistic pleasures of which I believed spoke to my commitment to life. Could a person who roasted three different kinds of apples for an autumn soup really be capable of suicide? I asked him this question laughing, wooden spoon aloft, during an argument about a drug I did not want to take. Doesn't the one cancel out the other, leaving you with a basically normal wife? They could delight me, my obsidian jokes, but he saw them hanging from me like statement jewelry, heavy, aggressive, things that could not be forgotten even as I spoke, quietly and practically, about the empirical world. He began not to trust me on issues I saw as unrelated: what a neighbor had said about a vine that grew up our shared fence, a letter from the electric company that I claimed to have left on his desk.

I passed through the contiguous rooms, high-ceilinged and white, as briskly as could be called civilized. Whatever my feelings about the work, I never want to be one of those people rushing through a museum, intent on immunity—I was here, their bodies say, and that was it. It is true I sometimes court discomfort, that I will deny my headache an antidote, and that I don't expect to feel the same way from one hour to the next. This was a quality my husband feared, then hated. That's the usual trajectory, it might be said. If we don't talk to the thing we are afraid of, it becomes the thing we hope to kill.

All the people in the room were young women, and I felt tenderly toward them, their damaged wool and winged eyeliner and overstuffed shoulder bags. They interested me more than the photos. What could I tell them, from just the other side of thirty, except that things did not seem to exist on the continuum we needed them to—so little of life was a rejoinder to something said or done earlier, the opportunity to, as school had often demanded, show what you had learned. Your real self was mostly revealed in negotiation with the unforeseen element. How did you behave when the emergency room bill arrived, triple the estimate? When someone you loved was suffering, how long did it take for you to wonder about a life that didn't include her? I had sidled up to one of them, the girls, whose face intrigued me particularly, a saturation of peachy freckles she had made no attempt to cover up. Hanging there, the object over which she was pouring her young mind, was my mother.

As far as I knew, my mother had lived in New York City for only six unfortunate months. The image I associate with them is not a photo of her looking bewildered by the Rockefeller tree or exposed on the steps of the Met—they don't exist—but rather a gesture she would make, at her suburban dining table, if ever asked to describe her time there: a low hook of the hand, swiped an inch or two to the left. Total dismissal. Sometimes, on the rare occasions she'd had more than her characteristic half-a-glass with dinner, a blush and a remark. I had no idea what I was doing there, she would say, and pat the hand of my father, the ostensible representative of a life she found a year later and understood quite a bit better.

About the photo in the museum, I will tell you this: my mother looks like someone who knows exactly what she is doing.

Seeing her like that, I started to cough and I could not stop. There is very little ambiguity about what has gone on in the pictured bedroom that contains her, shot from just outside it so that the leftmost third is a slice of peeling door, paint riddled with thumbtacks. There is the characteristic mattress, right on the floor, the open window and fire escape. There is some rubber tubing, knotted in places, elevated above the usual detritus on a milk crate. The inner sleeves of records, the cellophane casings of cigarette packs, a battered silk tie one must assume, from its crippled shape, has been used otherwise. That time passed for me, there in front of the photo, was a separate cruelty, for it came with no palliative or normalizing effect, and so the third minute I took it in elided with the ninth and the twelfth. A German tourist, the kind of spokesperson for a concerned and patient group of them, touched a finger to the back of my elbow. It was obvious, from the damp focus of their faces on mine, that it was not the first time he had spoken the word in my direction. "Please," he said. "Please," I replied, stepping back so that they could see her.

Though all identifiable marks were in place, the mole I had liked to press at the base of her jaw, the gap in her eyebrow from a childhood accident with the Girl Scouts, there was nothing about my mother's facial expression I recognized. It had not come up in her rare flirtations with anger, episodes about which she felt embarrassment for days. A faulty appliance without a warranty, a time I had, at fifteen, responded rudely to an elderly neighbor's offer of homemade rice pudding— Ev, whose teeth looked to me like towns devastated by hurricanes. Young lady, my mother had said, that the cruelest thing she could think to call me, your days aren't any bigger than hers. Even before she was ill my mother was a diminishing creature, eliminating distinctive or inconvenient parts of herself by the year. At fifty she stopped wearing the perfume she had for decades, her one luxury, thinking an insistence on a certain scent was an affectation of the young. What do people need to smell me for? she said, with a horsey puff of air out the side of her mouth. Once, from the passenger seat during a trip home, I watched her wait patiently while the man driving the car in front of us, by all observations asleep at the otherwise empty intersection, leaned farther across the wheel. Honk, I said, but my mother would not honk. Honey, have you considered he might need the sleep? Choose a radio station, for god's sake. There are some good ones around here, you know.

———

The Germans had formed a barrier around my mother, talking and gesturing, so I exited the museum, taking the stairs as my husband had always insisted. *A little bit of exercise* was a phrase he kept spring-loaded. The gap in our ages was hardly noticeable to others, and I had often imagined the point when the

stunning preservation of his youth would overtake the rapid
deterioration of mine. Growing up his beliefs as their rigidity
dictated, I was something like an espalier, the distance between
the vine and the thing that trained it almost imperceptible. I
wanted to call him, to wash his reasonable pragmatism all over
the issue of the illicit photo, but our terms would not allow it.
I can't deal with another crisis, my husband would say, the last
year we were together, in response to vexes I saw as relatively
small, a mix-up at the pharmacy over the drug I agreed to take,
some passive-aggressive email from a student I read out loud
in the kitchen, hoping to parse. I can tell you're in a state, he
would say, hands raised like an outdated television preacher.
Rather than responding to my speaking, he took to waving at
it, scenery to be considered later with the right amount of rest
and reflection.

I can't imagine the man, he said more than once, who
would have an easy time living with you. This hurt particularly, for he had a fabulous imagination—a jaunty talent with
a colored pencil, a habit of coming up with a song on the spot,
a fond feeling for the absurdity of animals. I began keeping a
tally of my behavior, days I had been so anxious at the incur-
sion of these thoughts that I wept or went sleepless, others
when my charm had been big and flexible. On a New Year's we
hosted, I built fantastical hats of construction paper and bal-
loons, things that looked like cities of the future. On his forty-
fifth birthday, in the park near our house, I hid his ten favorite
people behind his ten favorite trees, and guided him on the
snowy walk to discover them. I always scanned his face, on

occasions like these, for a look of recognition, one that would say, Here, here you are.

Contact between us now consisted mainly of three words, even the contraction never parted into its constituents. *Hope you're well*, he wrote. *Hope you're well*, I wrote. Hope you're well! Hope you're well! The statement never altered into a question, and with time it began to read to me as a kind of threat, beveled, ingenious. To his last *Hope you're well*, six weeks before, I had not replied, and I believed that was the end he had in mind. Pills in a blender with strawberry ice cream, I thought. An email scheduled a day ahead of time with very clear instructions. We had been separated a year.

———————

On the outdoor patio of the museum the tourists were unhappy, scratching their fat ankles, saying how far is it, how far, how much. It was midsummer, a time in New York I have always loved and dreaded for how it keeps no secrets, all smells and feelings arriving fully formed, unavoidable. I called my father. Since the separation from my husband he has been unsure of how to relate to me, in part because the small knots and amusements of domestic partnership were the only aspect of my life that mirrored any part of his. He had sometimes liked hearing what I was cooking, and always about the expensive and malfunctioning alarm system my husband had purchased. What, did it go off in the middle of the night again? my father asked once, excited enough that he was a little short of breath.

"Hey, it's me," I said.

"It's you."

"Do you know about this photo of Mom?" I referred to this without any introduction, I suppose because I felt I had been deprived of one and so wouldn't be offering such consideration to him.

"What's that?"

"There's this photo of Mom in a museum here."

I had to repeat myself several times, and when the point had been made and I had told him I was sure, he paused, the way he always did to gesture that my mother pick up the other phone in the hall. He could not kill the habit. I had seen this a million times, his left hand scooping the air up, the other pointer raised. She would stop whatever she was doing, leave the sentence unread, the sandwich half-assembled, so that they could hear together what it was the mechanic had to say, the second cousin with the coupon obsession. Visiting meant listening to the conversation of theirs that never ended, mundane talk that went on until they'd shut off their bedside lamps and sometimes after. Passing their room in the middle of the night once, I heard my father say, it must have been in his sleep, It's the damn compressor, and my mother reply, without missing a beat, You bet your ass it is.

"She was a looker, wasn't she? What is it, some kind of—do they call it street photography?"

"No," I said. I described in euphemism what was occurring in the photo.

"There's been some mistake," my father answered, finally, resolutely. "That's your eyes playing tricks on you."

It was one of a thousand precooked phrases he had on hand: canary in a coal mine, teach a man to fish, taste of your own medicine. Language to him was the same set of formations and markers, certain maxims always leading the way to others. After you pulled up your bootstraps, you reaped what you sowed. It was something he had adopted in recovery, I thought, the beginnings of which took place a decade before I was born. For my whole life, he had referred to himself that way: In recovery. It seemed unjust to me one had to adopt that title for the duration of living, but for my father it became a helpful boundary, a gate he could close on any conversation he wanted. As a child I had found the overheard expression comforting, repeated it to myself on anxious walks home from school. Thinking of a game whose rules I had failed to understand, the nubbly red Spalding that had flown past me, I would say, with mimicked weariness, You know, I'm in recovery.

He started to talk about television, a corner to which he often retreated when uncomfortable. It was a reliable tactic for how it bored and frustrated me, and ensured I'd be off the phone sooner than otherwise. "Well, there's a show you wouldn't believe," he said. "It's called *Naked and Afraid*. Well, they drop these people off on an island somewhere, and they don't give them any clothes." He always used that interjection, *well*, when describing something he was happy to have no part in. Shortly thereafter I said goodbye.

———————

By the next morning I had decided to email the photographer, but thought first I needed to return to the museum and take a photo of the photo. In the afternoon I taught, a creative writing workshop for people of nineteen and twenty, a task I could keep myself alive to only by pacing the rectangular formation of tables—as if by directing my voice from different corners of the room I had a better chance at some diplomatic pluralism in my thinking. We were talking about figurative language, and I wondered aloud how close a simile should get to the character's actual life and circumstances: in comparing her inner sadness to the color of her dress, weren't we depriving the reader of some useful speculative distance?

"No," said an opera singer with four names who despised me. "I literally love that."

There was always one student who hated me. This was a problem I could solve more easily with young men, pretending to lessen my authority while I sharpened my argument. But with girls it was never clear, for their hatred was much more original, multifaceted, and they clung to it even while enjoying whichever dialectic I'd introduced to distract them. They could entertain my line of reasoning while deriding the person beneath it. The opera singer had a habit, raising her hand against my litany of leading questions, of pointing out some aspect of my appearance. There's a hair on your jacket, your top button undone, that lace about to untie, a little something on your face. She made me wish I was only a voice, piped into the room and delivered by speakers placed along its windows.

On my way off campus, feeling comforted by the architecture and landscape, the Doric columns and rectilinear hedges, I called my father again, prepared to meet somewhere closer in feeling to him—accept his denial, and negotiate with it. No one answered the home number he'd kept, and when he picked up his cell phone he did so with an exaggerated element of surprise. It was clear just from the way he said hello that he was not going to acknowledge the conversation we'd had, that he'd hoped to forgive me it as he might anyone's spike in emotion, something attributable to hunger or fatigue.

"Honey, you ever wake up and want a hamburger so bad you believe you could will it into being? I finally gave up. I'm at the grocery store now, my poor soul."

"I want to apologize for yesterday," I said. "I hope I didn't upset you."

"Ants at a picnic," he replied. "You went with your gut." There was a slight delay to his speech, like he was trying to describe something moving to someone who couldn't see it, hoping to determine a pattern before he put it into words. When I began to continue he cut me off, telling me it was time for him to get in line.

———

In the last hour the museum was open, the exhibition was even more crowded, and I waited politely while a young couple holding hands observed the warped circle of my mother's mouth. The thoughts had not totally ceased since leaving my husband, but because there was no one else to assign them any importance, they were less of a source of alarm. I have a friend who lives in an apartment where the door can be opened only with a wrench, but it doesn't keep her from leaving. Anything can be lived around, so long as it's only you who has to do it. The betrayal of my mind, when we were together, had seemed to my husband like a betrayal of him, of the life that looked like a happy one. A hotel suite uptown, I thought, a maid you'd somehow apologize to beforehand.

———————

My husband had met my mother just once before she was ill, a lunch where he had paid and she had been impressed, and then he knew her for the five weeks she was vanishing. Despite her embarrassment at having to die, she was generous about allowing him into it, often saying how nice it was to be spending so much time with him, and he was saintly with her, crushing her pills into water when he saw swallowing was an issue, making sure she heard her name spoken lightly. These were the sorts of problems he took to with alacrity, ailments and logistics, a crooked angle or a smudged glass. To this day I cannot look at a man who is looking at a map, for it recalls him so totally, how happily he believed in things reduced to their signifiers. At first he delighted in my missing sense of direction, asking me with wide eyes where I thought I might be going, but in the end it infuriated him, the time I might take for just any left. That's not teaching you anything, he would say, when I raised the map on my phone to pull up a list of directions. Did he believe a certain native impracticality of mine was part of the same looseness in the world that made me want to leave it? During trips he'd spread a brittle map on the trunk of the rental car and say, Just take a minute alone with this. Tell me what you think the best way is. Perhaps he thought the problem was margins, that if I could better plan A to B in the physical world, avoiding tolls and traffic, then in my mind, too, I could ignore the periphery. A downtown six you might leap toward like a deer, I thought, pliant, ready for what it would do to you.

That I had never "tried anything"—this was the phrase that he used—seemed to me to be an obvious point of credit, a spotless record that pointed to more of the same. Of course, the thoughts had disturbed me enough that I had confessed to having them, about a year after my mother died, in the dark after sex in the middle of the night. This was the time he wanted me the most, calling me in from where sleep had taken me, his body my reintroduction to the living world.

I had hoped that if I let the thoughts into the room they would lose some of their power, a kind of blackmail in the way they were invisible to others but kept my life on a leash. I would have two drinks but never three, accept a compliment but never believe it. Though he was warm and soft when I first confided, the separative effect I had wished for, some congratulations I might receive for naming the thing that hunted me, did not take shape. Instead, my husband began looking for cohesion, seeing any dip in my feeling as proof of the roots the thoughts had taken in me. If I was quiet at a dinner somewhere, despite the light being good and the weather lucky, my forehead might as well have been a projected strip of celluloid bearing the ghastly imperative: k i l l y o u r s e l f. What is it? he would say, his mouth firming up and his eyes losing a little color. For god's sake, what are you thinking right now? Once, because I had only been remembering a college friend and her peculiar party trick, a dancer who had smoked cigarettes with her toes, I snapped. Strictly of your happiness, I said, holding up my empty wineglass as if to toast.

———————

I was able to contact the photographer only through a friend of mine who taught at the university where she sometimes lectured, and he warned me Sam Baldwin was moody and unlikely to reply. She conducted famous seminars on her own work, performances I'd heard described once as a whole child-hood, meaning every possible emotion, meaning each pared to its loudest part. People said she'd lost her wire-frame bifo-cals sometime in the mid-eighties and since wore her prescrip-tion sunglasses, which she removed just to shoot. *Good luck*, he wrote, and concluded his email with a typo of omission, the question, *Are you feeling?* to which I responded only, *Yes*.

My note to her was brief and included the photo, which had not otherwise been catalogued and was scarce and low-resolution online. I explained the situation and asked if she'd mind telling me anything she remembered, about that day or my mother. My phone rang within the hour, while I was observing a pickup game of basketball at West Fourth Street, my fingers threaded through the diamonds of the fence. I like watching the minor parts of the body during moments of leaps and stretches, acts we think of as the jobs of legs and arms. The cut of an ankle as the foot rolls, ball to toes, upward, or the hip bone exposed to sun for the instant, mid-dunk, when the shirt rises up the ribs. I like to be inside the shouting but silent to it. This was something I did that I told no one about, a whole hour unaccounted-for, and it was one of the great pleasures I'd experienced since leaving my husband, a certain thought ringing like a bell calling me in: nobody knows where I am, nobody knows where I am, nobody knows where I am.

After clearing her throat excessively, as if alone in a room, and unwrapping what sounded like three small candies, the photographer asked if I'd like to come by sometime that week. She lived a few blocks from where I stood then, a fact I decided not to mention. It seemed a step had been skipped in resolving the distance between us, but I agreed, my mind still half-tied to a swiveling calf I saw through the fence.

———————

The day came to see her and I could not decide on the appropriate clothes to wear. Finally I decided on a jumpsuit, sienna, linen, which made little about who I was easy to imagine. The building, once industrial, was air-conditioned in the way of a car dealership. She opened the door coughing, rolling her eyes at her body and gesturing with the hand not covering her mouth for me to come in. The apartment was cluttered but not unclean, the feeling being that the stray books in stacks were often removed and referenced. Pointing at my shoes and the straw mat where I should place them, she walked toward two cracked-leather egg chairs that faced one another under a skylight, and I followed. She was not wearing any glasses. She was speaking through the middle of a thought she had begun without me.

"And of course I was so glad it was included in the retrospective," she was saying. "You know, the pieces of mine that gain some valence, the ones the most reproduced, often aren't the same I would have chosen. Funny that it wasn't for so long. I guess a woman taking the thing she wanted, a man doing something for her, was never as interesting as the alternative. Funny that was your mother. I liked her."

She didn't hesitate in the transition from the talk of the photo to its subject. The way that she poured the tea, a minor flourish of her wrist, into two Japanese mugs without handles, made me feel vaguely guilty about the way I'd dismissed her work. As it was steeping she got up—distracted by a memory, I believed, ready to pull out some arcana that would help her comment—but then she was drawing something around my shoulders, a knit blue afghan, imperfect, smelling of smoke.

"You're supposed to ask people if they want to be taken care of, isn't that right? I'm sorry." She rolled her eyes again, this time at her instincts. "She came the first time it showed, wearing a pantsuit and pearls. We all loved that. Irony was not valid for her. She thought, Well, I've got my picture up at a gallery, I better look like a taxpayer."

Something in my face must have changed, because she put a hand on my knee.

"Did I?" she said. "Is there?"

"I didn't know she knew."

The photographer watched me figuring out why this mattered. It was clear she had a way of encouraging a person's natural state, even becoming a part of it, by goading on any reaction, turning the room to its expression. On the table between us she set a ceramic Kleenex holder, and then she moved about opening the windows to the noise from the street, bringing the heat in and making the throw around my shoulders irrelevant. I couldn't help believing she was the reason for every feeling I had, the comfort but also the anger. A bay you found lovely to begin with, I thought, a bridge in the afternoon. The color changing with your view of it, the depth uncertain.

Why did it matter? I had wanted to believe the photo was taken not of my mother but from her, a thing she would not have given freely. I had wanted to see it as an exception. I asked the questions I did next without totally asking them, maybe so I could convince myself later that the photographer had told me things I never needed to know. Sitting back in the chair with her tea held halfway up her body, the photographer mentioned that my mother had been the girlfriend of a friend of a friend.

"I remember loving the way her face and body reacted separately. It was like the body would tell the face what was happening and the face would say, Are you sure? She had her days-of-the-week underwear soaking in the bathroom sink, which broke my fucking heart."

When she said this, what came to mind immediately was another photo of hers, one of the most famous. The soiled pale pink, the shallow basin of water the hue of disintegrating leaves, the elastic losing its threading. W E D N E S D A Y. On the mirror above are phone numbers in eyeliner, a long-antennaed cockroach crawling over fives and sevens. I was waiting for her to expand upon this, to attach her memory to the abbreviated public record of it, but it never came. It was as if she had seen as much as I had, could speculate about the lives behind the torn faces in her work no better than anyone else. If she knew she was not sharing an anecdote but referencing a canonized image, she gave no indication.

The silence that ensued was like a change in weather, something that rendered us powerless in a way it was hard to take personally. I would ask nothing further about the woman in the photo, the splay of her knees, the delicate bloom of a bruise on her inner elbow, just visible in the way she gripped the man's hair, and the photographer would ask nothing at all about the rest of my mother's life, not even her name. "I'd love to shoot you sometime," she said, after the disappointing moment had turned over, and I said only, "Thank you," a response as vague as it was insincere.

When she closed the door behind me it was easy to believe that it had never opened, that the apartment was unknown to me. In the jerking elevator down I sent my father two texts, one the photo of my mother, and the next a part of it I had zoomed in on and cropped, the distinctive split of her left eyebrow. I understood how the conversation would go, and I was using a tack I knew would aggrieve him, preempting his protest. I walked along Sixth Avenue and into the first movie I found, an Australian art-house thriller. A middle-aged couple wearing the colors of hard candy had kidnapped a teenage girl, a blonde in shorts that crossed her ass at a mean diagonal. The camera loved the wet line of her teeth, wanted to move all the way down them and into her throat. It was scoreless, the sounds of her torture off-screen the subdued soundtrack to what happened on-, where the husband or wife persisted with the domestic, pouring budget cereal into plastic bowls, filling the water trays of their twin Dobermans. In scenes across town we saw the pale back of a mother's neck, the fallen elbows, while she looked through her daughter's possessions for a sign of what had driven her away. The handheld shots suggested a state of watching from another room, without the desire to enter or the resources to leave.

———————

When the movie let out I saw that my father hadn't responded to my texts, so I sent two more, words this time, *What do you think?* and then, *Well???* They did not show up as delivered. The evening was dark enough that it felt physical, a deepening of color that came with a smell and a taste. I had never known my father to turn his phone off, and in fact would have imagined he did not know how. He spent most of his truant feeling on it, revisiting the photos of cracks in the wall to be caulked, tapping at the weather icons of cities he'd visited once a long time ago.

An email from the photographer appeared as I stood in front of the theater, in view of the basketball courts that were empty now. Devoid of people they looked liquid, interruptions of pure space that did and wanted nothing. The email referenced neither the minimal conversation we'd had nor the complicated one we'd avoided. *I'd like to shoot you sometime*, she had written. *When can I?* A gun shop, I thought, where you bantered a little outside your politics with the owner, some bald man with ideas about a woman's instincts for self-preservation, who congratulated your investment in personal safety.

I could tell by the way my skin felt, inadequate for the task of holding in everything it had to, that I was going to call my husband. Like anybody about to break a law, I felt a thrill at the decision I'd made—that, however briefly, the rules did not apply, that I was free from the forces that had circumscribed me. With each ring of the phone I imagined the different places he might be, at the counter of our neighborhood Italian restaurant with the long, mirrored bar, in bed with a girl who laughed at everything, on line at the airport with his rolling titanium suitcase. That he did not pick up did not surprise me, but that there was no response to my transgression saddened me. I wanted to hear his voice snap at the line I had crossed, to know what he thought was selfish about the thing I needed. I called him once more that evening, and sent my father three more question marks. I did not respond to the email from the photographer. My mother wrote at eight-thirty, asking if I was feeling alone. There were many people nearby, young, single, possibly naked.

In bed at night I thought of the last hour of my marriage, which had unspooled, in predictable irony, the morning after a wedding. I had arrived to the breakfast first, at the Hudson Valley farmhouse turned rustic inn, to the row of carefully distressed tables along the porch. My husband had stayed in the room to shower and shave. Waiting for him with another couple, acquaintances who coordinated their clothing and spoke one another's names so often it seemed part of a prenuptial agreement, I looked out at the spread of hills, a green that was nearly uniform. When he appeared I watched him walk toward and then past me, forsaking the seat on my left for one at the empty table next to it. Embarrassed for me before I became embarrassed for myself, the couple exchanged a look. They straightened their silverware. They spoke one another's names.

A half an hour later, on the unmade bed that looked like an envelope torn open, I mentioned the chair I had saved. I used the word *divorce*. My husband accused me of looking for symbols where there were none, and then I was blithe as I'd rarely been in our time together, packing up my weekend bag, checking in the morning light for what might have been forgotten.

———

In the studio apartment where I'd moved to be alone, I woke the next morning to a call from my father, the fourth in a row. In the background there was the sound of wind or water, in his voice a kind of directness that would have frightened me as a child. He asked if I'd had my coffee yet, and said he would wait while I made it, asking nothing after that, none of the little questions that buttoned our conversations together: hot enough for you, how's the city so nice they named it twice. I told him I'd need to put the phone down a minute, and if he'd rather I could call him back, but he said he was happy to stay on the line. As I boiled water and dumped yesterday's grounds from the French press, I kept looking at the phone where I'd set it on my small, high table, in the shadow of a copper bowl where I'd floated white carnations in water, worried that whatever he had to say would change given how long he had to wait.

When I finally settled on the stool I put him on speaker, wanting, in some childish way, for his voice to fill the room. I could imagine his exculpations: that she had been one in a million, full of surprises, and this was just another, bitter a pill as it was to swallow. So long as he accepted the most critical fact of it, I was prepared to give him every sympathy. I would offer never to bring it up again.

"First, I want to apologize," he said. "I never expected this to come up, and I guess I thought I might be able to push it back down."

"Of course you didn't," I said. "How could you have expected it?"

That I had spoken did not seem to matter. I had the sense, for the first time in my life, of what my father was like alone, fearful because he was brittle, unhappy because he was fearful, determined because he was unhappy.

"She never told you about that time in her life, and I believed that was her choice and her right."

I looked for his voice on the petals in the water, in the crystals of salt I kept in a low ceramic platter.

"Are you saying you knew about the photo?"

"I didn't know specifically about the photo, but I knew about the circumstances surrounding it. When I met your mother she was nine months clean and I was six, and she still had some New York on her. Crosswalks were invisible. If somebody said how are you, her shoulders went up. She'd done it cold turkey, no program, no rehab, nothing. That impressed the hell out of me."

"But she drank," I said. "What about the sauvignon blanc at dinner? Aren't addicts supposed to—"

This question, as with all others I asked in the brief remainder of the phone call, my father answered in as few words as possible, denying me any real information. My voice spiked and flew and his refused to meet it. In dismissing my catechism, he was returning her to the place where dead people live, her mysteries as irrelevant now as her peanut allergy or pilled lilac robe. I wanted to believe that another conversation was happening inside the one I could hear, that maybe, in allowing my mother her life, protecting it from my revisionist inquiries, he was reminding me of the rights I had, the questions about who I was or how I suffered for which there were no categorical answers. By the time my father said goodbye, the noise had grown around him, busy, total, and I said, vaguely irritated, "Where are you going, anyway?"

"I'm going to the goddamn game," he answered, knit so deep into his living that he did not think to tell me which.

————————

I responded to the photographer sometime in the surreal afternoon that followed, a time in which all my thoughts felt half-
lit, things that had belonged to someone else and which I held
up to test for an emotion I'd know when I found it. There were
certain memories of my husband I had never revisited, a night
I had let a moth into the bedroom and he had been viciously
annoyed. I had been reading, but he insisted we turn out all
the lights and reopen all the windows, tempt it with the glow
of the street, and while we lay waiting for the thing to fly out of
the room I could feel his palms pressing on the mattress, taut
against sleep or comfort. I did not cry out in satisfaction at its
exit, as he did, and I could tell my silence bothered him, even
though the sheets were clean and soft, even though the smell in
our home was of spring. *I'm open to being photographed*, I wrote
to the photographer, *so long as I'm asleep.*

A field, I thought then. A yellow caned chair. A room up
some stairs that was empty.

A WORLD WITHOUT MEN

◆

They had been singing the same songs at the same bar for forty-two years, she dyeing their hair the same box-black for twenty-three, when the virus shut down Los Angeles. The last Saturday before the closure, plenty of young people were still out on the East Side, touching each other in the semicircular booths of maroon vinyl. Frankie and Shirley did "Bewitched," did "Unforgettable," her teeth biting a smile as she blasted down the keyboard, his drum strokes fluid as he sailed elsewhere in his mind. The few who could recognize his fine training forgave him his distraction, and others were less generous. The martini glasses floated up; the tip jar went around; the drunk young man pulled out his phone to photograph them, as one always did. Frankie stood from the drum kit and aimed the flashlight into his vision, making other people laugh, though Frankie did not. It was the final performance of their career—"See you tomorrow," they said in unison—and everyone assumed that only death would part them.

In the refashioned broom closet, a space Shirley had petitioned to be done with new paint and mirrors, she dotted Pond's under her eyes and asked him if he thought she'd put too much oomph, too early, into "Mack the Knife." Pulling on his gray sweats, he cupped her shoulder. They left through the back door and got into the Corolla, Shirley honking "A Shave and a Haircut" as she clipped a curb on their way home to Venice. If she was less bothered by their station as hokey representatives of the twentieth century, it was perhaps because her power in it had always been an ersatz version of his, and she had taught herself not to distinguish the real from the fake.

The call came the next morning. Having just worked the dye along the white line of his roots, she stepped out of the bathroom with the chalky gloves on. He listened to her take it, the coolness of chemicals piled on his scalp still a kind of thrill as he sat on the pink-cushioned toilet. Pain, for Francis, had always been an acceptable substitute for pleasure. She came whistling back through the door she hadn't shut, saying the bar was temporarily shuttered while they got the bug under control. Drawing from her reserve of maladapted optimism—the certainty things would get better because they almost never had, and a greater force might finally take notice—Shirley told Francis that they would be back to work in two weeks. He winked in response, an acknowledgment so automatic by now that it seemed almost biological.

When the timer went off and she told him to rinse, he stood under the showerhead with his hand vaguely on his cock. It was an area for which he had something like a tourist visa, free to sightsee but not take on any earnest work. He thought of his plane's drag over Hanoi, a girlfriend whose stammer vanished in the bedroom. Three bags of spinach, Shirley was saying, beyond the curtain, two of oranges. She recited the contents of their refrigerator and freezer, then years of nonperishables stocked in the pantry, calculating a trip to the store could be put off a month. Her confidence, her way with a plan, had always been what pulled them through the material world, and his talent had been what pushed them. Theirs was the only band in the world where the drummer played lead, and the rest was backup.

They spent the next weeks in front of the television, flipping mornings between *Good Morning America* and *Fox and Friends*. Sometimes Shirley would make a call to her sister, in a home in New Jersey. Francis, who had no family left, started standing by the opened front door. He liked looking toward the light from the ocean, and the idea that if someone came too near, the mailman or a dog walker whose animal veered onto the lawn, he could erase them immediately by shutting it—look the threat in the face from his three-steps-up vantage, throw a wall between him and the unknown. Under his bare skin, the cheap flat of metal that bridged carpet and concrete was hot and a little cruel. They had lived in the apartment since '73, accepting the hour-long west-east commute, with the offer of the gig in '78, as part of their American life. In the earliest days, she did it all before they got in the car, baubles, hair spray, the extreme undertaking that was the transformation of her face, and as he drove he could feel her makeup bloat in the sun a quarter of an inch in every direction. He had worn aviators to dull her sequins as much as anything.

By the middle of the third week of the shutdown, she announced they would need to practice their act.

No drums here, he pointed out.

So do it with your hands, she answered.

They went out to the back patio, five-by-six feet of concrete that abutted an overgrown lot, and she set up her keyboard. She sang to the honeysuckle that grew through the chain link, picking a flower between songs and turning it between thumb and index like it was a prize. She brought the blossom to her face and huffed it, explaining that *this* was the *life*. That was how she survived, naming what was banal a bit of luck, a dispensation that pointed to further rewards. The right parking space could carbonate her mood for a whole day, some fries left off the bill would let her know that her god was a good one.

Behind her on the metal chair, he was completely still. If he had once admired that quality, it was the kind of admiration that serves as a weak explanation for lust, and it left when the lust did. Because they were people without children, the desire was never replaced by anything else. He had wanted one, a son who'd idolize him or a daughter he'd worship, but when the topic came up, she brought out the bank statements. Show me, she had said, the space in the budget for a nightly babysitter. He had not broached the topic again. Leaving her to sing "Unforgettable" to a fence, Francis went inside to stand by the open refrigerator. In the deeper circles of his self-hatred, he felt sure he was the same as the parking space—the same accident in her life, mistaken for the same divinity. When they met, he had been thirty-two but living like someone younger. In a bad furnished room that he'd taken sight unseen, his dog tags stayed snaked six months on the windowsill, exactly where he'd first dropped them. He had spent the year after his discharge drumming for a Liberace impersonator, getting stoned out by the trash so he could stomach the wretched meals the restaurant gave the band.

When it came time for the next dye, Shirley woke up at quarter after nine and took her coffee to the bathroom. He was standing at the opened front door when she called his name, and he did not immediately come, nor answer. What are you doing, she called, where's Frankie? After a long time he replied, but his voice went out into the world rather than back into theirs, and she couldn't make him out. On the bowed false-wood bookshelves were her crime novels, her erotic novels, her plastic boxes of less-used jewelry. He kept little of himself around and always had, even his drumsticks slipped somewhere she didn't know or think to ask.

In the fall of 1972, staring at him where he stood by the garbage, she had the face of a deer but the presence of a tank. And who's this? had been her opening line, winking and coming in through the back door with a girlfriend. No fuckin' idea, but I'll check, he answered, which made her grin. Three weeks later he invited her to his puce room and played her a less-appreciated Beach Boys record, his way of making the place beautiful. Sitting on the mattress not touching her, Francis said he loved *Wild Honey* because it was as scary as it was happy. He pointed out the unusual exaltations of the organ, and she coiled the dog tags, neatly, absently, never asking permission, earning his total gratitude. *I'd love just once to see you in the nude*, harmonized Mike Love with the Wilsons. Taking this as scripture, she removed her green dress.

For a long time, that memory would run to him as happily as a child to a parent, as if asking to be praised or corrected, sometimes surprising Francis by teaching him about himself. Then it stopped coming. If he invoked it on his own, the meaning had changed, or there was no meaning. But the fact that he had written to a friend the year they met, admitting how she made him want to make music, write it—that was never really gone. This was less a memory than some words printed on his life. To enunciate your desires, he would have told his younger self, was a punishment that came back to you later, shaming you in your own voice.

When he finally appeared in the bathroom, he took his dutiful seat. You look dreamy, he heard her accuse. Out the small open window a jacaranda budded, and he knew what purple litter it would leave on the sidewalk. It was obvious to Francis how many in the audience, night after night, liked to guess at the dimensions of his happiness. He had enjoyed knowing they came to different conclusions, believing that made all conclusions possible. It alarmed him, now, that he was the only one in a position to speculate.

———————

Shirley drew the comb through his hair, tugging the white of his roots from the pink of his scalp, already feeling the chemicals working in her own plastic cap. Squeezing the plastic

bottle, she was remembering how, walking the beauty aisle of
the Safeway for the first time, he had held up dark browns and
coppery reds. It's cheaper and easier to be the same, she had
said, tapping the obsidian black. She'd invested in bulk scrubs
shortly after, and they each wore them now, the plasticky sea-
foam paper spotted with their most recent dyeings.

She'd always been the one to know what they could afford,
though occasionally she'd let him spend as wildly as he was
inclined so that he might suffer the consequences. The June
he'd impulse-bought a Harley, they'd eaten olives and jam for
two weeks till he resold it. The fall the coke habit became a
little more than that, she said nothing, awaiting the moment
when this would ruin a set and instruct him, which it did.
She restrained herself when he was intent on sabotage, having
learned early that to broker another way, to suggest she help,
risked enraging him. Pity, to Francis, was a four-letter word.
There was never a right answer with his spectacles of despair:
when she held out a hand he found reasons to hate the fingers,
but in withholding help she became associated with his fall—
she was the person who watched his disaster. His anger came
only in spells of frozen silences, which seemed to convince him
it was not anger. I love you, she had been foolish enough to
tell him, in the half-life of one of these episodes. That's your
own poor judgment, he responded. He had a rule, anyway,
about those words, which Shirley would have liked to use in
the place of "sweet dreams" or "good morning." He would say
them once a year, no more.

Moving her fingers around his left ear, Shirley told him

again how soon they would be back to work. Before you can say boredom, she said, and she believed it, having no other option. She took in few of the shocking headlines, preferring spring in California, a report she had always believed in: there were joggers out there, she could hear them panting by, and cars that still played music. There would always be the Pacific, would always be that other country at the edge of theirs, and she believed without thinking much about it that the virus couldn't live on the ocean, would be peacefully extinguished by the symphony of light and heat and water. This was a bleached-out hunch, something like her whole life here. She was third-generation, she told people, explaining if they got nosy that her hometown in Arizona had been a part of Spanish California. Besides Frankie, she said, her love in life was the ocean, which, she often repeated, was the biggest thing you could touch. She said the same things in different conversations, in part because she was accustomed to giving the same performance twice in a day, in part because she had never believed much in her mind, and felt the people she talked to deserved the best she'd put together.

When she had secured them the gig, he was deep in his thirties. Though she knew this was not what he'd imagined, in his wish to make a living as a musician, Shirley believed in bargaining, even with dreams, even if those dreams were somebody else's. And for a long time it had made him happy, the routine, the drink tickets, the Disney animators who came from their Atwater studio to watch, then shake his hand. There were sometimes bit parts in B movies, there was always their name on the marquee. At home in bed, Francis had behaved like the veteran he was: crawling onto her expecting to be saved by duty, all purpose and expectation, then changing his mind halfway through, behaving as if they were subjected to a sudden threat, then as though she were the threat itself. A hand over her mouth, Don't move, stay still, then tightening just slightly too much around her throat. She had imagined there were many women who liked this, and she believed she was something like most women. Trying to tell her sister about it, she gave up. It seemed impossible to explain that he had been somewhere else, hurting something else on another plane and so not really hurting her at all, and beside the point to mention that their performance the next day—charisma flowing from her keyboard to his drum kit—was once-in-a-career. If she had gone to college, she thought, she could have explained it in a way that was tidy, but if that was the point of college, that was probably what was wrong with the country. They were registered Democrats when they met, both vaguely pacifists who regretted what the war had done to Francis, and what it made him do. But Carter was a disappointment, the lines at gas stations during the second oil crisis all the proof of that she needed. In '81, at Shirley's insistence, they swung to Reagan. He'll keep the lights on, she had told Francis. Typically, he did not agree or disagree.

She checked over his left side and was about to start on his right when he put his two hands up in a cross over his forehead.

Finished, he announced. It was all he would say.

You're only half done, Shirley said. She bent out the cabinet mirror and pointed. He wasn't looking that way, was removing the scrubs and stepping into the shower, onto the rubber strips she'd paid a neighbor to apply. Stunned, she waited, imagining the correct invective. When he moved the curtain aside she gasped—the water had made the interruption of color even uglier. He looked like some animal removed from its native environment, the victim of strange weather, ready to consider anything as food.

Privacy, he said, reaching behind her for a towel.

It was a word she had not heard spoken in their household. In their early years, he had followed her into every shower, asking her, grinning, how it felt to have a pet. Decades in, he still insisted she stay in earshot, insisting when he pressed tulip bulbs into their front yard that she set up in a plastic chair nearby. The change in him now was as real as architecture, nothing she could see through to the other side.

When she got May on the phone a few days later, Shirley tried to tell her about the hair dye episode, but Frankie's behavior seemed irrelevant next to what was happening to her sister. Some of May's friends had been taken from the home by children concerned the bug would spread there. "Agnes left yesterday with her granddaughter and a cheap valise," May said. "Last I talked to Karen, some daughter she is, she was sad about the cookout she throws for Greg's company."

Shirley wanted to say something about the antidote of the ocean, what it could do for your health, but she did not have the phrasing down yet. Maybe her sister would fly out here, she thinly suggested instead, just in time for their first performance back, and they'd dedicate a song to her. "I don't know about that," May said. Dinner was ready, May announced soon after, and got off the phone. Shirley felt her pulse, then passed into the bedroom to change her jewelry, thinking she needed orange instead of olive, thinking she'd feel better with Lucite than wood. Frankie lay atop the made bed, engrossed by the television. She ran her hands over the jewelry trays on her dressing table as an announcer described the conditions of a reality show: twenty-five people had been left on an island and told they could not have sex without facing a punishment.

This isn't entertainment, it's the fact of life for most men! Frankie boomed at the television, though he did not change the channel.

But he had been the one to put an end to that, she thought, telling her when she tried to peck him in the kitchen, not long after he turned sixty-five, how that was something he no longer did. It was supposed to be a good year, the first they qualified for Medicare, dental to boot. When a heckling drunk in the audience had demanded they kiss, she had cheated out her shoulder and hair, leaned in close to make it seem they had. She was protecting both of them from what the world wouldn't understand, she told herself, even as she admitted she did not understand it either. What did a single kiss cost him, for what was he saving?

When she exited she closed the door, turning on the living room set to drown him out. On it she watched the President deliver a press conference on a cure for the bug. Heat and light were powerful in killing it, he said, and she snapped her fingers where she sat—it was like she had thought! She and the President of the United States had the same idea. The thought appeared as quickly as she sent it away: in a world without men, I would have risen to the top.

Three hours later, when he sat down to dinner of pasta with canned peas, she tried to speak of this coincidence but he waved it away, looking like he did when he dismissed a beggar. She leveled a curved pointer at the white stripe that moved roughly from his forehead to his nape. Skunk left for dead, she clarified.

Then he was as quiet as he took vicious pride in becoming— he could stay silent for days if he was hurt or angry enough. Once he had left his plate in the sink and scuttled back to bed, she faced off with the clock on the wall, scowling because it made her think of where in their act they'd be. That's amore, she said. In the alcove off the pantry, where they kept the computer, she sat down and pressed power on the modem. When the screen was blue she pressed CHESS. There was maybe some gunk in the mouse, and that made it hard to move her pieces where she needed them. When the computer won, it played the trumpet.

She cried briefly in her chair in the living room, thinking how all she wanted was to tell someone about the virus, about the stay-at-home orders, and have that be the first they'd heard of it. In an emergency, in a crisis, she had always measured her reaction against the face of the person she confessed it to, and readjusted given their calm or alarm. But the virus had happened to everyone, and rather than making her feel more connected to all life, it told her that the small details of hers didn't matter. She moved then toward the front door, opened it, and stood on the jamb. Shirley stayed there fifteen minutes, trying, as she always had, to understand how he felt without being able to ask.

———————

It was time to get groceries, she said, the next morning, the moment she opened her eyes. They'd gone a month without. All his life it had been this way, she waking up to tell him what must be done. He wasn't ready to be awake, deep in a dream about a wolf he wrestled at the head of a forest, some vestigial language from a Boy Scout manual coming to him as he pried the mouth open, feeling the place where fur met gum. *He is loyal to all,* he said into the blue eyes, as frightened of him as they were aroused, *to whom loyalty is due!*

Oranges, she was saying. Spinach, mouse traps, Pond's. The window was cracked and he could feel the salt beyond it, the bedroom was cluttered and he could blame her vanity alone. On the duvet cover the fleur-de-lis in gold had baked, over two decades, into a fecal mustard. She was speaking again of his hair. Could they fix it before going shopping? If all her life she had woken up afraid, ready to please, eager to *do*, what responsibility did he have?

Staying inside made her nervous, but he had started to like the quarantine. The lack of an audience had scared, then freed him—no more gin eyes, no more vodka smiles, nobody looking at him but his wife, and even that he felt he could eliminate. He was making himself unsightly to her, he was disappearing into his mind. He understood totally, once the realization came to him: in all the flashes of public solitude, his fingers pressed down the neck of the stand-up bass, his drum fills that reduced the room to only that sound, he had been practicing for this. It was like a sign said, nearby on the boardwalk in a restaurant window: YOU HAVE EVERYTHING YOU NEED. He thought it again and again, not as a message just received, but a fact he had, until recently, forgotten.

He dressed without answering her natter, pulling on a pair of pants that had sat in a drawer for decades. They were the pure yellow of a toddler's urine, high-cut with sailor's pockets and white candy buttons. The scoop-neck T-shirt he slipped into—SECRETARIES DO IT WITHOUT ERRORS, it said—had been forgotten, too. *Go without me*, he wrote on a Post-it in the kitchen and pressed to the fridge. At the door he slipped into boat shoes with orthopedic inserts, and he left it open when he went, moving west, toward sun on water. Whatever war had done to him, he was glad to have flown above ocean, triangulating toward the docks where he'd make his landing, feeling as rich, and as vanishing, as the light he raced over its surface.

In the songs they had sung, the world was about timing and luck: a room flattened by lust to two people, a past erased by a plane ride somewhere else. But he had come to understand, by the faces he played to, that these were phenomena as out of time as Shirley's false lashes. As Francis kissed the hi-hat the phones raised and lowered, saying a man was as diffuse as the reach of his technology, that distinct places were no more. He could only hold the flashlight up so many times per night. There was always someone stealing his image, dispatching it to a broad network of everywhere and so nowhere. The phones made no difference to Shirley, who had never been her own, but to him they said: you belong to other people. To Francis they said his life could be understood in his absence, laughed about and relayed to anyone. That was far worse than dying, a last act for which you received, in apostrophe, some hushed congratulation.

By the entrance to the boardwalk a man tanned with dirt hacked as he bit a skunky joint. His possessions were around him on a bench, a sleeping bag and a cross-eyed husky and *The 4-Hour Workweek* in crumbling paperback. "I'd like some," he said, and the man hesitated. But maybe his surprise at being approached, after a life in which he'd lived under the world and not in it, felt tantamount to his consent. That was something Francis understood. The man handed the smoking thing over, asking Francis if he'd heard about the virus.

He coughed as he drew the smoke in, but that didn't stop him from another pull.

"Here it comes," Francis said, referring to what he wasn't sure, and handed the roach back as he floated toward the blue water, past signs that called the beach off-limits, taking his shoes off, then his pants. Sitting down on a slight hill, Francis poured sand from his clenched right fist to his open left palm, then reversed the role of the hands. The ocean had no ambition, he thought, and he admired the hell out of that.

———

Shirley drove back from the grocery store with her palms sweating on the wheel, reminding herself of the freedoms men had always required. "Boys will be boys," she said aloud, trying to remember if there was any exemption, on the other side, about what girls would be. She had tried to call May, when she found the Post-it, but there was no longer any answer at the retirement home's front desk. She had not worn a mask at the store, reminding herself, when she saw so many, the similar interruption on different types of faces, that neither did the President.

The red and blue lights she saw from down the street, but she did not consider they might refer to her until it was unavoidable. Frankie stood dripping on the lawn in only a towel and his gold chain, two policemen in masks standing six feet from him and from each other, making a triangle on the lawn.

"Is this your husband, ma'am?" one said as she parked, popping the trunk to lift the groceries out of it. "Reported for his presence on the beach."

"A big personality, all right," Shirley said, which she understood from their faces was not the correct answer.

"We can carry those groceries up the stoop for you," one said.

She thanked them as Frankie passed inside, stopping on the step to reach into the rosebush, where they kept a key always hidden in a wooden matchbox. *Love is a rose but you better not pick it*, went a song he had liked by a folk singer she despised. You can play it when I'm not around, she had said, knowing full well that was almost never.

He sat in his chair without the television on as she put the cans and bottles away. She made herself a plate of sardines on toast and took it into the bedroom, where she watched reruns of *Dancing with the Stars*, calling out the missteps as if she were a judge, and fell asleep that way. She dreamed of life in her body as it had never been, unqualified by other people. Shirley was alone at the barre, kicking a leg behind her like a prize horse, and every mirror reflected her. When she woke to Frankie standing over the bed, she had that embarrassment of sleep about her, and when he climbed on top she laughed like she had at the tricks played by her brothers—the pretty doll roasted in the oven, the bloodstained panties on a dinner plate. It had been twelve years. What a surprise, was the last real thing she said before he started.

There was so much she would have done to prepare if only she had been warned. There were so many things she would have wanted if only she had been asked if she did.

———

It didn't feel like it once had, and whether the lingering high helped or hurt he debated as he moved, keeping his rhythm. As he did while drumming, he understood that every note he struck had its vital half-life, attack and decay. My love, she called him. She made ugly noises, she spoke his name. Speak your own name, he thought, and closed his eyes. His erection was not for her, it was for the future. All told it took five minutes.

Well, well, she said. What else do you want you haven't told me about?

This he considered in earnest. He was seventy-eight years old, born in the interregnum of generations and belonging to neither, and as a child he had been allowed to decorate his own room, going with his mother to pick out new wallpaper, new lampshades and curtains. As a quarterback he'd been famous for his pivot, as a pilot for his carrier landings. The point was, he knew he could take a turn, could stop on a dime, that you could drop him anywhere and he would know which way was north.

I think a divorce, Francis answered.

Shirley laughed and told him he was acting crazy, and he reminded her of the line she'd spoken to crowds when he introduced her as his better half—we've been together forty-five years, and they were thirty of the best years of my life. Lying back, he mentally catalogued his things, the containers he could use to pack them. He slept that night in his chair, which went nearly horizontal if you pulled the wood lever. When he woke to her standing over him, sometime near dawn, he closed his eyes as soon as he'd opened them.

They didn't speak for two days. At the end of the second he turned on the computer, the first time he ever had, though he'd watched her check their email—set up, she said, for fans. He'd had no use for the internet, did not trust it as a place you could not exactly go and never exactly leave. As it whirred awake, so did he, remembering watching her search for lyrics, once they had floated the idea of adding some new songs. *Realtor*, he typed. Images of bleached teeth multiplied in front of him. *Room for rent Venice*. Many answers, insane numbers. She paused behind him on her way to start her decaf, and he lifted the mouse like a remote, pointing it at an image of some inlaid shelving. The shadow behind him vanished, and when she called to him from the kitchen he turned his hearing aid down. He returned his attention to the task of packing, opening a suitcase on the bed before deciding on a walk. But the air didn't feel the way it had when he'd sat on the beach, amenable, and he ended up at a bus stop only a block down, watching the sky through scratched-up yellow plastic.

The bus in Los Angeles was a nasty rumor: for years you heard of it, never hoping to investigate the truth of it yourself. Almost all the seats were empty when he got on, and as he pulled out his billfold to pay, the driver said something through his mask that Francis didn't understand. The driver gestured toward his face, but Francis took his ticket and sat down. The one other passenger, a woman in scrubs, had a long look at him, and he thought maybe she had seen the act. People often recognized the two of them, and it was a nice way to move through the city, the smiles of strangers. The bus took them away, and that felt good, and he pointed at his fellow passenger.

"I've got a pair of those," he said, leaning across the aisle, pointing at her scrubs and then at his scalp, "for reasons of beauty." She looked unsettled. He looked out the window at California, streets whose names were famous to him. Ten minutes later, a mother and toddler got on, and the woman in the scrubs began to speak to them in Spanish, wincing and nodding. Though the women wouldn't look at him, the little girl did—a perfect thing of two, dress a birthday cake, ears already pierced in gold. Another passenger got on at the next block, this time a man in a shirt that said MCDONALD'S, and the woman in scrubs spoke to him in English.

"They got you working?" she said, her voice pitching up.

"Drive-through," the man answered. Francis kept his eyes near the floor.

In his line of vision the girl stood between her mother's knees. She had on a little mask, but he could tell from her eyes she was smiling, and he was smiling, too, waggling his eyebrows as he might onstage. At a wide turn she took two steps toward him, the dark wisps around her face parting, and he saw the disaster before it happened, the chubby ankle, the tiny foot in leatherette unsteady: her mother was a foot away, so he would be the one to save her. But as he bent to reach there was shouting—the mother saying don't touch her, the woman in scrubs saying don't touch her, the McDonald's employee with his phone up saying the virus, saying don't touch her—and then it was as if his body objected. He ended up instead on a hip on the floor.

Few of the noises, after, applied to him, he thought, the child as she cried, the mother as she soothed, the neighbor as she stood by concerned.

"I'm going to lift you from behind, sir." He refused and he refused loudly, getting himself onto all fours and then reaching for a pole. It took too long, hand over hand up the hot blue plastic, and once he'd made it up he never sat back down, waiting for the next stop and then getting off. Maybe he'd see a FOR RENT sign on the way home, he thought weakly, and turned in that direction. He hadn't made it far.

He never really caught his breath from all the ruckus. He tried to hear it as happening in two/three measures, which made the labored sound of it less frightening. After the virus, would there be music in the same way? Two two three. Not songs for other people, not for a long time, not even, really, the theater of conversation. There would not be wits exchanged over sweating glass, there would not be the good scarf for the airplane, for that way of living had already been on its way out. The smoke coming off the twentieth century, decades which had made the senses their topic, had lingered for twenty years. Now it was gone. The virus had removed the distractions of novel color or breeze or percussion, diminished anyone to what he had been avoiding. Here, the disease said, are the plain walls of your life.

Breaths he began to think of as individuals, each with its own recalcitrance. At an inhale he thought: nice to meet you. He felt a resistance that seemed to come, if possible, from outside his body—light he passed under wanted to strike him, space he moved through refused his path. He had to stop a few times, and the afternoon was hot by the time he reached home. From a few houses down, he could hear her flute, see the high angle of her elbow in the window. That was all of life to her. Something for which you kept practicing.

When he tried the door it wouldn't. When he reached for the key it wasn't. On the frame was his own handwriting, *Go without me*, but circled in red, and with the addition —*Shirley*. Putting his hands on the railing to lower himself, he noticed that he could not smell the ocean. He yelled it then, the word he felt he had always known. Shirley. Francis looked around him then, down the street where he had belonged, someone who knew the life spans of trees and the brave names of dogs. In his life he had been lucky, forgiven—known as a man in his triumphs, understood as a boy in his mistakes. He had loved a woman because she was going to make him better, and he had stopped when she couldn't, and now even her own name, called through her own house, would not bring her.

PART OF THE COUNTRY

♦

In that part of the country where I tried to live alone, the burned-out California of nobody's dreams, I measured time in the disappearance of roadkill. A deer on the shoulder took less than a day to be removed, a raccoon at least a couple. Braking around the curves in the road where these shapes remained, I spent my idle thinking on the barking dog. Each night, the noise seemed not to echo through the redwoods around my property, but come amplified, and encircling, from them. By the time I abandoned that house, a damp place of warped decks and spectacular views, I was sleeping little more than three hours a night, and living like prey under the threat of something bigger. Even now, I don't think I could describe the sound of that dog, menacing and pitiful, though I believe I could make it—it sometimes happens that we're afraid of a sound because we know, somewhere in our bodies, is the same one.

A county over from the house were the remains of a town a fire had erased the fall before. I drove through it only once, turning left at cinder-block foundations already white with sun. Twenty minutes in the other direction, another had flooded so badly that the stop signs, in the photos we'd all seen in the news, appeared halved. Joseph, hearing where I'd bought as I packed my things—I meant it as a surprise for the both of us, I'd told myself the seasons before as I skulked real estate late at night—peered at the photos and gagged. *Do you hate your life,* he asked, *or just your money?* But the house, the warming planet, did not seem to me so much bigger a risk than many I'd taken with my safety: to love a person born with the privileges he was, for instance. This was something my mother had warned me about, the spring I met him, but by then I saw her advice like something in the back of a fridge, likely past its expiry and suspect anyway for how rarely one had reached for it.

————

I arrived in the country still spotting—in rare cases, this can last weeks—with a skillet and a tape measure and the kind of delusive optimism that only kicks in when rational attempts at peace have failed. My first week there, I baked cornbread and read poetry and purchased, from an antique store lit only by sun, a box of strangely colored tile. The rectangles were marbled green and pearl, patches of pink or blue coming through in some but not others. There were more important repairs, a faulty fixture on the kitchen sink the previous owner could only have installed on meth or horseback. But I focused first on color and light, installing those tiles above the bathroom sink and dimmer switches in the bedroom. I crouched and reached, blew and twisted, and walked at dusk to the river, where I swam against the current, an argument I always enjoyed, and always lost.

There was not a part of my body I did not use, the first week. I slept very well despite the heat, which was dry and somehow red, the same color of the dust it lived in. Problems that could be solved with a screwdriver, or by money paid to some contractor, made me happy that September. When my new used car developed a strange cough, the hassle of bringing it to the mechanic didn't bother me. He had been the closest option by far, and had responded to the message I'd left on the shop's machine with emoji-infested text messages. *I'll put your fire out*, he had written, followed by a squadron of flames and blue droplets and body builders with dumbbells.

After the first time he fixed it, he let me know about surviving a shooting at a garlic festival, pulling up an article on his phone that showed him fleeing. "Zoom in," he'd instructed me. "It just goes to show you," he said, widening his eyes, and I averted mine, worried about what he believed this might demonstrate. I spent the next three hours at a bad diner down the road, a pleasant interruption of microwaved pie and carton milk. Though the look the mechanic gave me when I returned was too long, the alcoholic heat coming off him too pronounced, I was able to forget it the moment I drove away. "Come back soon," he called, that day or another, which I did find an odd injunction.

Can a dog make the same sounds, beaten, that it might on its own, suffering? I woke to the noise, the first time, around five a.m., unfortunate timing given how it coincided with sunrise, leaving me to think, as I gained consciousness, that one had somehow created the other—that the sweep of pink through the window was the face of that yowling, that the cry invented the light slipping through the trees. I'd gone to bed around midnight, and decided not to sleep any longer, trying to make virtue out of deprivation.

It's true I could have communicated better with my husband about my decision, the two pills I took—the first at the clinic, the second a day later—but I worried he would convince me otherwise, Joseph, whose mind was the first thing I loved about him, and also the first I hated. My feeling for him ruled me, but a vestigial boarding-school Catholicism ruled him. It was an occasional fever that charmed me at first, as unkempt and godless as I'd always been: the way fear or faith would land on his face. Our first autumn together, he once turned on a heel, gasping at the entrance of the train on a morning we were both late, and said I should go on without him. We had forgotten to make his bed, and he could not face the idea of abandoning that sin.

Joseph and I had met on the subway, something that might seem romantic until you consider how faulty an introduction that is, with no chatter of commonality, shared friends or culture. Any love we wanted we beat our way toward alone, laughing, not worrying enough about the distance between our native minds, the advice each of us had been given before we were old enough to qualify it. Wasn't it funny, he of a Notting Hill childhood and starched Eton puberty, next to a girl from somewhere else completely, raised by a single mother at free clinics and public pools? I delighted in the Milton he could recite from memory, the print of his education on his thinking, and he in the questions I didn't bother to ask: could one disregard that sign, decline that invitation, swim in that body of water. *This is* classic *you*, he would say, following me into whichever forbidden passage. Once, seeing me dressed in white in October, he put an index finger to my shoulder and said, *I'm no Connecticut dandy, but after Labor Day?*

That's a rule, I'd replied, *for people who never have sex for any reason except "it's nighttime."* Joseph repeated my remark into the gingkos as we left the house, squeezing my sides. *Clever girl*, he said often, *my clever girl*. When we discussed my mother, which we almost never did, he was sympathetic to my situation, if perhaps too eager to summarize it. He spoke of how I had, in his words, clawed my way up, how I was, in his terms, a real American, self-made and self-governed.

When I brought a photo of her to him in bed once, having found it in an old suitcase the night before a trip, he looked a long time: at the way she lifted me to the sun by the river, at the leotard she wore instead of a bathing suit, at the Coke in her hand and Camel in her mouth. Then he put it down without a word, as if to say: what's to be done? The fact of my body separating from hers, thirty years before, was the only piece of information he needed. It was an expression I'd seen in the courtroom, where in our earliest love I had gone to watch him—the performed silence, the buttoning of his lip. I'd do impressions of him later, when we were naked, mocking his

outsized sincerity, purposely invoking the wrong Latin, and
he'd gasp in disgust and delight and beg for more.

Remarkable, he'd said, that night he saw her photo, patting
the bed beside him.

Her? I had asked, still standing, grinning at the suggestion.
You.

———

On a run I took in the afternoon, I jogged in place by fences
where I saw a dog, looking huskies and boxers and pit bulls
in the eye. A bark is supposed to be distinctive, but whichever distortion—the distance the sound traveled, the pain the
creature was in—had made it impossible to identify the round
vowels of a hound, or the emasculated yap of a terrier. Passing a wan green house where a fungus of snouts came through
the chain link, I believed this ruled out all of them. Wouldn't
one dog, barking, incite another? It did not seem possible they
would refuse to comment on its suffering, if only to reprove it.

The sounds of the dog were worse the next night, and
started at twelve-thirty, so after some hours awake I began a
painting project, a shell-white to cover the antacid-pink in the
second bedroom. My breathing, I noticed, was shallow, my
grip on the brush uncertain. As though it were something I'd
learned but forgotten, I tried to identify what I was afraid of:
not really the dog, not really the house. It was not really even
that part of the country, where the cursing that came through
the trees, over coupons not honored, rides not offered, seemed

likely to result in violence, and the things I saw on the check-out belts of the grocery store, fourteen of the same canned dinner, made what I put in my body seem excessive and strange.

Though I managed the first coat neatly enough, finishing at three-thirty, I found the next day that I'd somehow tracked paint down the hardwood flooring of the hall. Living alone for the first time in years, it was alarming to know every mess was mine: I'd see the many cabinet doors I'd left open, the spill I'd left to clean until later, and think, *That's you, that's who you are.* As I crouched to feel the braille of the paint bumps, a text from the mechanic came in—*how's the car cupcake*—and I swiped left to ignore it.

Around three that afternoon I made my way down the steep grade of the twisting road, stepping sideways toward the fence where I'd stopped the day before. The house it protected was built on stilts, as were all of them in that neighborhood. This produced the sensation of being watched from above, and also the suspicion that when those houses fell, their disaster would include me. The dogs all gathered in the area beneath a bloated patio, where a trellis supporting it seemed ready to give. Eyes of chlorinated blue, coats of rust, six of them or seven: I felt ashamed, somehow, of why I had come, and spoke to them sweetly before I mounted the stairs, before I rang the bell, one of those vertical buttons whose tinny sound feels less like a *hello* than a *thanks-for-nothing.*

"The fuck is that," hissed a voice from inside, and I took a step back as I heard the catch of a lighter's flint.

———

By a year into my relationship with Joseph, I had stopped
answering my mother's calls. When the question of family
came up in public, he helped me evade it, keeping the question
of my past away as he pointed to the riches of our future. *Have
you got a big family, Claudia?* some acquaintance of his might
say, and Joseph would laugh and sling an arm around me: *She's
certainly going to if I have anything to do with it.* About the cold
country that had grown between my mother and me, he was
supportive, telling me we can't help who we come from, only
who we become. Later, in front of a friend of his, his closest from Oxford, he asked my permission to speak of it. *She's
ghosted her mother, George,* he said. *Have you ever heard of something so American?*

My distance from my mother was not a matter of comfort but necessity, I thought, an evaluation I paid a therapist
three hundred dollars a week to confirm, in an office that
made it obvious which language to use. The guilt I felt, the
way her need punished my achievements. Sitting in that taste-
ful, expensive room, I cried often, recounting memories of
my mother mere minutes after I'd ignored her call. Jeff the
therapist nodded, smiling occasionally with his very bleached
teeth, telling me I was brave, rolling closer in his chair if my
sobs became deeper. Would I like a hug, he would ask, and
if I agreed I spent the nights until the next session googling
different versions of the same question—*can your therapist
hug you*—changing the phrasing because sometimes I wanted
the internet's supportive yes, sometimes a resounding no.

Gestalt therapy + *physical touch* + *depression* always brought a better answer than the plain, dumb question.

————

The woman answered the door followed by a rolling oxygen tank. I could see her husband in the background, smoking, tapping on his phone. Introducing myself, I apologized almost immediately, so that it emerged seeming like part of my surname, I'm Claudia Sorry. I told her I was a new neighbor, and she asked me where I worked.

I'm a designer, I mentioned, I work for myself, understanding immediately this was a mark against me, in her eyes, a sign I only trusted myself, and was not to be trusted.

"I've been hearing this barking at night," I said.

"Probably a dog," my neighbor replied.

"It's keeping me from sleeping," I faltered. "I wasn't sure where it was coming from, but I thought I'd see if it might be one of yours." Fussing with a button on her oxygen tank that deepened its hiss, she paused to look at me in the light that was changing. Sun reached that street only between two and four, and by six the place felt again like a child's neglected terrarium, a place for frogs and moss and standing water.

"My dogs have a good life," she said. There was the flint of a lighter again, and a male voice asked who it is was. "It's Claudia, the new neighbor. She works for herself." Then she started coughing and laughing, and I left as I'd arrived, apologizing.

"Come around again and I'll do the barking, honey," she called as I fled down the stairs. The dogs, as I passed, were

silent, though the minute I'd moved out of view they all began
to bark. Feeling shame infested with anger, or anger infested
with shame, I took another way home, stopping near a house
just painted a pleasing kind of yellow, and stood in its empty
driveway. In a window that was wide and clean, a tawny mutt
sat on a couch, the room around it dark. When it saw me, it put
its paws on the sill.

————

Two weeks before I had swallowed the misoprostol, at a dinner
we gave for a friend's birthday, I heard Joseph repeat something
I'd said verbatim, a remark I'd made about the early American
fondness for the Greek column—a gaudy celebration of democ-
racy that raised a finger to Britain. He delivered the line better than I had. Standing at the sink, I sifted my mind and felt
similar memories falling down it, a time at a holiday party that
something I'd read and summarized for his amusement came
off his tongue, delighting the circle of people around him. I'd
been across the bar, triangulating a grip of three cocktails, and
when I returned to his side he passed one to his colleague, but
did not introduce me to several people I hadn't met. On our
walk home he held me in such a particular way, an arm around
my waist and a hand slipped under my braided leather belt,
that I could not imagine breaking the warmth there to say or
ask anything in particular. *My brilliant girl*, he called me, that
night as he fucked me, praising my mind as he made himself
at home in my body. We had whole conversations that way,
pauses where we stopped panting to talk over some drag or

gleam to the day, a tiff we'd had or a painting we'd loved. If I thought that was communion, if I thought it meant some merging of souls, if I thought there was such a God-issued thing as a soul: I did not really consider what the force of him did to the remarks I made then, whether I assented to his line of thinking because it seemed to come from inside my own body.

When I took the test that confirmed what I suspected, Joseph had sat opposite me, against the bathroom wall, his feet threaded through mine. *Baby*, he said, looking at me with the kind of pride reserved for great achievements, and there was not a question between us of what we ought to do. I did not think much of the fact that I had not seen that expression on his face before—on the occasion of a prize I'd won for a hotel I'd redesigned, silk curtains dyed naturally by the area's rain, or a grant I'd received for my study of organic iridescence. Later that week, we attended a third birthday party for his colleague's twin daughters, Lucy who insisted on a lilac tutu and a veil, Naomi who straddled a rocking horse and asked boisterous questions.

I was rude to anybody who spoke to me that afternoon, so intent was I on watching Joseph with those girls, newly three and loudly alive. From the deck I craned my head, turning back to watch him through the sliding glass doors. Lucy, who held a wand in one hand and a face-paint grease stick in the other, stood on the dining table where he must have lifted her, the tulle pushed back from her face. He sat in the chair, his eyes closed to her transformation of him, and she was silent and gentle, rendering him in silver and blue. I was moved by his happy calm, a phenomenon from which the whole future issued, certain and mine. It brought to mind a memory of him, the summer I'd sprained an ankle in Italy, carrying me piggyback as he called *Fate largo* through the twists of Venice, allowing me to dictate left or right by a pull on the corresponding hank of his hair. I returned to the conversation around me for a moment, and when I looked back again I saw Naomi at his foot. She wore a sheriff's star, and giggled as she tucked something in the cuff of his pants, then sat on his suede oxford. Asking Lucy to pause a moment, he reached down, picked up Naomi, and placed her a few feet away, displacing her cowboy hat. It was brusque but not quite violent, cold but not quite vicious. I was the only one to see what had made her cry, and also that he ignored her tears.

─────────

When I reached the house I stepped in my car immediately and drove to a drugstore, where I bought earplugs and the kind of antihistamine that warns the user about operating heavy machinery. As I paid the cashier, he asked how I was spending my day, and I told him I had some projects at home. He nodded, and I returned the question, practicing a generosity with strangers I had spent ten urban years eliminating. He told me that every Sunday he and a friend went to a movie, which he would that night.

"You know what we call it?" he asked. I shook my head.

"Movie club," he said, and we each smiled, though not

exactly toward each other. I returned to my parking space, and as I put on the news I saw a text I'd missed. *Nevermind don't bother replying just saw you driving you look very happy*, wrote the mechanic.

I had no plans to respond to his message, but as I started back I heard it—the cough again, a squelching when I turned the key in the ignition. Though I'd delighted in the prospect of car ownership after so long in the city, and had not even tried to bargain with the man whose ad had read "or best offer," the liability of it came with an element of fear. It was like taking responsibility for a whole other body, any problem that cropped up likely indicative of five others, and I had dreams about it most nights, an indication on the dash I hadn't heeded. It occurred to me the mechanic had enacted some kind of quick fix designed to prompt my return, and I heard Joseph's laugh in my head. *Lovely as you are*, he would have said, *do you really think the man has enough mental pennies saved up to focus on you? He's not planning past the next PornHub search term, darling, and even that's not terribly original.* In the last hour of daylight I spread newspaper on the deck and began sanding a chair I hoped to refinish, which was not the most practical, given that the wiring out there was faulty and the light wouldn't work. I rubbed down the last leg in the dark, trying to tell myself I would know the change was enough just by the feel of it. It had been a season since I'd left him, and there seemed little point to it, given how clearly I could hear his thinking, and how easily I could push it into mine.

––––––––

Joseph had come home from work the day after the party with a bouquet of peonies, asking what I'd thought of some article he'd emailed. *Come, now,* he said, when I was silent, *we both know you're going to have something smart to say about this. Is it . . .* he asked, placing a hand on my abdomen, then after what I needed, a seltzer, a bath, a foot rub. When I mentioned what I'd seen of him with the girls, careful to keep any thought of what it meant from escaping, he anticipated my worry and laughed, a kindness coming into his eyes. *Darling,* he said, *you're worried I only want a little princess? Don't be foolish. How could that be true, given that I've chosen you? I wouldn't put it past you to skin a cat and eat it, if we were desperate. It's part of why we're together.* His laugh was like the British sound of the word, fuller than my laugh had ever been, more credible. Joseph took me in his lap and I pressed further, asking about the weeping he'd ignored, but he put a hand on my forehead and asked if it wasn't true that Naomi had stopped with her fit soon after, likely as a result of the fact that he hadn't fussed over it. *Not every feeling,* he had said, *is deserving of a seminar.*

––––––––

The antihistamine I took, that night, put me to rest if not to sleep. I felt as I sometimes had in sex with Joseph, that my body existed for the sake of something acting upon it, that it was happiest with direction. When I heard the dog through the drug, I believed I deserved it, that I had changed my life and these were the terms. In the sediment of the next morning, I found the website for animal services, then the section in which I could *Report an Issue*. Under issues, there was *Barking Dog*.

Type the address of the barking dog, it said, to which I typed *uncertain*, then *many*, then *not applicable*. Finally, I called the number, saying to the man who answered that the corridor of trees both obscured and amplified the sound, making its source unknowable, that I believed there were either several dogs or a dog in such distress the sounds it made changed, and that I heard these noises only at night. When I was done speaking, he paused.

"And what's the address of the barking dog?" he said.

"The dog has no address," I snapped. "I only know its position as relative to mine."

"We aren't dog detectives," he explained. "Don't really have the time to be lurking on streets at night, waiting to catch a clue."

"I'm sorry," I said, though I very much was not.

"Don't be sorry, just be certain," said the man, and I went out to the deck. I could tell that the work I'd done, in the compromise of what I could see, was uneven. What I needed was to be somewhere else, so I got in the car, but the coughing, this time, would not stop, and the car would not start. I tried to call the mechanic at the shop, but there was no answer, so I sent a text.

———

In the fallout of our conversation about those little girls, Joseph had been tender and quiet for most of two days, asking about the looks that passed across my face, taking a handkerchief from his pocket on the summer evening when something in the weather made me cry. It had been a stiff August, a month for which my body always kept some fragile anxiety—a transmission from grade school summers when I would fall asleep rearranging the off-brand pencils and folders on my twin bed again, imagining the performance I would give, unforgettable to the teachers I worshipped. We were passing down East Houston, headed toward a movie. I felt a sudden fear about a life without them: movies, matinees, hours that could shape me without my shaping them. Hadn't it closed too quickly, the window of freedom? I had been a girl in a classroom, alive to the questions of other people, then a young woman in a bar, budgeting another drink and a walk home or to spend it all on a cab right then—and after that, only briefly, had I been just a person. For about five years, I'd possessed enough money and confidence that most bad turns of luck or circumstance could be made or unmade with the correct remark or payment. For about three of those five, I had worried neither about the theater of my girlhood, the shoddy rope swing in my front yard whose arc I furiously repeated, or the decades in front of me, years which I'd never really bothered to imagine beyond a general change in posture: the way I would bend toward the need of a child. Touching my face on the street, Joseph laughed, not without love. *I don't know about you, darling, but I still plan on getting to the cinema quite a bit. In your imagination, what's happened to the sitters?* He found the place in my back where he knew I'd been sore, and he pressed his fingers along it. Soon we were walking again, soon we were at concessions, and he bought us popcorn and bonbons and sparkling water. *Kiss my nose*, he said, as we stood in a line that was beginning to move, *I won't budge if you don't*. Absurdity like this was his way of erasing everything around us, reminding me of my belonging. I rolled my eyes but he tapped his right nostril with a slapstick solemnity, and by the time we were seated I was laughing into his shoulder.

In the dark of the theater, feeling warm in his gestures of comfort, I tried to remember when he'd last allowed me to provide him any comfort. In London two Christmases before, I had caught him frozen at the doorframe of the front room where his father sat playing Rachmaninoff. Through the windows came a crystalline glow from the square across the way, the last hour before his mother would walk through the house, switching on the lamps with her fine fingers. Thinking Joseph had been moved, I took his elbow and murmured something admiring, how his father's left hand flirted down the lower octaves, convincing them. But he flinched my touch away and marched down the hall, saying there was something off in how his father played, a hesitation there hadn't been in Joseph's childhood.

He had spent the two weeks there taking sudden turns into unused rooms of the house, moving a chair back to the way he remembered it, cursing quietly about any deviation from his boyhood that seemed permanent. These changes he consulted his mother about at dinner—a certain painting new to a room, chinoiserie vanished without his consent. When I asked what was on his mind, on a walk we took after brandy by the fire, he made a dismissive wave. My questions had seemed to Joseph invasions of privacy, and I hung back to watch him move ahead through Hyde Park, passing into snow where dogs flew silent, the only interruptions to fields of white.

Toward the end of that trip I had called my mother, something I did not tell Joseph. *It's . . . my . . . peaches!* she said, like a game show host. *You caught me right after I'd stopped betting on it, but I knew it'd be you eventually.* There followed a few tentative conversations, over the next two months, in which I had skirted the details of my life—where we'd bought, how we'd spent Christmas—and asked as few questions as I'd answered. Then I had offered to buy her health care, a thousand a month with dental included, and she had stated plainly that she'd rather have the money, told me about the bills she was not able to manage.

When I made my airy argument about the resources replenished by a healthy life, about there being different kinds of wealth, she said I was as far from understanding her as the sea was the shore. *Tell me what that even means,* I yelped, thinking then was not the time for her barstool poesy. *You're bigger and you make me smaller,* she said, and hung up the phone. The calls I placed after that went unreturned.

————

Maybe half an hour after I'd left the mechanic the message, a tow truck I hadn't called came, arriving at the same moment as a text from him—*tow en route no charge let me know ur safe*—and

I watched as the man mounted my car on his bed and took it slowly away.

I looked up at the house, then, from the empty driveway beneath it, and saw it differently than I had when it was a structure I might easily speed away from. I could replace the cheap windows with thick old glass, I could rip out the deck and put in fresh cedar: it would still be a place built on stilts, under a lacework of thousand-year-old shadows, where the question of disaster fell under when, not if. And then, in answer to the question he had asked a season before, I wrote to Joseph, breaking the silence.

Maybe I hate my life too, but you're the only person I know who doesn't hate his money, I wrote.

Practice makes perfect, he responded instantly, and I was sure he knew it made me laugh.

I left for the day right then, deciding I'd walk the three miles to town, and from the slim shoulder I called my mother, an activity that had become passive and almost soothing in the year since she'd answered. Her voicemail greeting was a recording of her boyfriend, on an untuned piano, making up a song about her name. He was a musician she'd known when she was much younger, and she'd moved into his cheap rental on the outskirts of Sacramento. The once I visited, just before meeting Joseph, I'd watched him drink eight beers over the course of two hours, forgetting what he'd said the minute before but never to light her cigarette. *You should have seen your mother*, he said, when she was in the bathroom, a thought on which he did not elaborate, an obligation to the past I had no way of fulfilling.

Rather than reaching some finality of expression in the way that she aged, my mother looked like an unfinished version of herself, thin in strange places, the colors of her face only half filled in. She could think of little to ask me, except for money, and I could think of little to ask her, except a vague forgiveness, for what my mind changed every day. College and graduate school, pleats and watches, the Ubers I called from, all the parts of my life that said something about the way she and I had lived together. Bedrooms we had shared in scanter years, just-bought secondhand shoes already half-dead when we slipped them on with stagey exclamations in the car. She'd cheered my progress from the sidelines until a certain point, likely until the moment she understood there was no finish line, that the sprint went farther than even I could see.

Watching me pack for a semester abroad, she had stood by, grinning. *I'm so excited, I feel like I'm going,* she had said. We stayed up until two, in the motel room by the airport she had splurged on, smoking the cigarettes I had not yet quit, giving each other pedicures, talking out the arguments with our boyfriends of the moment. Then we kissed good night on the mouth and linked pinkies as we slept, the last night it was true that any place known to one was known to the other. I did not send a postcard, that trip or the next, telling myself a beveled lie about it—that the risk of envy, when I told those stories and described those places, would be better mitigated by a squeeze of my hand, the foreign element naturalized, as I spoke of it, by the familiar story of my face.

————

When Joseph had left for a bachelor weekend, seven p.m. on a Thursday, I was eight weeks pregnant, and when he returned Monday evening I was a shape on the mattress. That I did it in private seemed important to me, proof I had chased an outcome on my own recommendation. The pain was not so much more than I felt in other months, though the mess was surreal, a study in color that changed each time I looked at the towel underneath me. *You could have told me*, Joseph said, wilted at the foot of the bed, a statement to which I did not reply, because one point of my many was that I had not drawn a curtain often enough, between us, that there was nowhere—in my past or my future, my love or my anger—I had not allowed him. The Vicodin was a benefit, something that helped me through that talk. I was able to tell him about the hate on my mind without resenting the creature it had made me. He wilted when I told him how he felt about women, he sat on the floor.

I had never been able to resist his hair, chin-length with a shine to it, the only part of him that was free, but as it moved around his face I looked instead at the city out the window, thinking about the world I had kept her from, my daughter, the streets of buildings all designed by men, the achievements of stone and glass in which she would not see herself reflected. *We couldn't know yet it was a girl*, he reminded me, and I nodded, softening a minute as he crawled onto the bed. *But a son*, I pointed out, *would have watched you with me.*

Joseph's mouth was wet, as he held my hand, saying please, begging for what I didn't know, just to be let back into the time before I believed these things about him. *Baby*, he said. I remembered the first time a man had called me that, a musician with a tender, studied curl of a bottom lip, and how after I'd told a girlfriend, holding her hand as we passed from a train station up into the street. We were twenty-one, still using makeup to hide how recently we'd been girls, and we said it over and over again to each other, what he'd said inside me, *Little baby, little baby*, cackling. Our certainty—that we would never want that comparison, that love when it came would arrive with respect—was big and round, a force circumscribing us. I don't know when it changed, just that after it seemed the most minor of concessions. If I had to endure the interrupting colleague, the doctor whose hand stayed on my back too long, then maybe to be named that, by the men I had chosen, was a correction for the rest: being called something less so I'd be given something more. I lost track of that friend, though I had seen online she met a man and took his name, a fact no one could blame her for, for the one she'd been born with was slight, if not ugly.

————

In town I walked to the shore of the public beach, a place where a labrador had died the previous summer from a neurotoxic algae, a result of the water's higher temperature. It was the sort of place that had a beauty if you looked up and out, but not down and around. Nearby a couple argued by the half-inflated raft they'd arrived in, she stomping a tattooed ankle that read *I Just Can't Seem to Drink You Off My Mind,* he waving a twenty-two-ounce can of beer that he finally crushed between his hands in emphasis.

I was on that beach, I told myself, I was alone in that town, because I'd made a choice—to give up my daughter— or because there was a choice I refused to make: to protect her, over and over, from threats as they became more complicated. A text from the mechanic came in, and I squinted in the sun to read it. *Where are u beautiful*, it said. *I'll bring the car 2 u.* Watching a hawk that circled above the trees, I tried to forget the strangers, their argument, but then I was caught even on my classification of them as such. It was an odd idea, that anyone familiar was worthy of more trust. "This is just like you," he was saying, as though that were the ultimate insult, and I saw she was walking toward the path with her hands raised, like someone indicating she had no weapon.

Please don't call me that, I typed. *It makes me severely uncomfortable.* I lay back rigid in the sand, trying to disarm the sides of my vision, sensing that if I turned at all toward the man whose girlfriend had left he would have a word for me about it.

K, texted the mechanic. *Maybe u wanna call the guy u bought the fucking car from bitch at him about your car trouble not the guy who helped u out of pocket with a tow when u buy a car u know nothing about.* The phone died as I typed and deleted.

————

When I arrived home, sunburned and emptied, the car was waiting for me in my driveway, the mutt I'd seen in a window days before pacing above on my deck. The keys weren't in the ignition, I saw, then passed up the swollen stairs. Sniffing at the swollen wood, its paws bloated and knees white with age, the dog had the air of a substitute teacher, doing something so that it could not be accused of doing nothing. When it saw me, there was hardly an acknowledgment. I followed it around, trying to get its attention, and when my greeting became exclamatory, when I yelled, *HEY*, it finally turned its head. In that state of little sleep my thoughts had largely changed from interpretation to narration, and as I followed it I thought, *You're following this dog around your deck. You're following this silent dog. You're not going inside. Why aren't you going inside?* And when the answer came, I knew it was correct and I knew the way I was starting to live was not. *You're trying to get this dog to bark at you*, it said, and I saw that was true. The keys were not in the mailbox where I hoped they might be. I left the dog on the porch.

Inside I plugged in my phone and turned on the shower. I wanted to remember nothing, as I imagined sometimes Joseph must have—that he would step into warm water and see only into the future. When I emerged there was a text from the mechanic. *Hi cupcake I didn't mean to snap just a stressful day long hours heavy tools I'm here to help not to hurt accidentally run off with your keys tell me when I should come by anything u need just let me know.* I did not respond, just crawled into the unmade bed with the towel still around me.

When the knock came, an hour later, I was asleep at the bottom of the world, and I pulled on stained jeans and a T-shirt from the floor, the first things I could find.

I knew who it must be. That the mechanic had come seemed inevitable to me, and I grabbed my pocketknife from the top of the dresser where the clutter of my life had begun to accrue, thinking I would hold it in my fist as I demanded my keys and his silence. The blade was clean and lucent, leading me by the kitchen where I saw cups I'd left unwashed, through the foyer where a debris of greenish pennies lined the sill. But the face through the screen was another man's, kind, open, though bent to something behind it: the dog, which he held by its collar. I set the knife on the windowsill, I tried to forget how it had felt.

"I'm sorry," he said. "I saw your husband bring your car in an hour ago so I figured you were home. This guy's been wandering a lot since we moved in, and he seems to like your deck. He's half-blind and half-deaf, but it's made him more adventurous, not less!"

His laugh invited mine to join him, as the dog licked his fingers, and though I knew there were polite questions I'd been trained to ask, I could not even hiss how that wasn't my husband, so transformed was I still by the feeling in my body— remanded to violence, ready to jump.

"I promise to be more respectful of your privacy in the future," he said, retreating from the door as I stared him away.

It was a perfect apology, dreamed up by corporate method, the self at the helm and the past beside the point. I began to pack that evening, all my things dirty.

————————

Joseph always sleeps well, no matter the circumstance. Now, on the nights I cannot, I pass through the black of our house, getting to know the things I belong to just by their feel. I can sense a wall without touching it, meet the last stair on the way down with no surprise. It was not a shock to him that I returned home, he said later, when I mentioned it was to me, perhaps hoping to communicate that my inner life still tendered some threats. I had not called him until after I'd booked the last-minute ticket and taken the cab ride, thinking of many men in that backseat. There was the tall college boyfriend who fetched me from work in his immaculate Mercedes, taking me back to his front porch, where I drank on his lap until he carried me inside. The reporter whose stormy moods I worshipped, arriving the moment he met a deadline at the restaurant he specified, staying as still as he asked in the dim light of his bedroom. As for the checks I never reached toward, the doors pulled open before me, anyone would have guessed I enjoyed that, the way I had shone and pressed myself, after, to lapels in thanks.

The fall I returned to him, Joseph took the C to JFK and met me at bag claim, where my luggage came quickly and he placed it on a rolling cart. In the dark of the car, the driver a part of the silence, I summarized my position: we could return to what we were, I could love him as I always had, so long as we agreed against children. As we passed down the remote avenues of Queens past advertisements that did not apply to us, for discount furniture and payday loans, he was quiet a long time. Then our neighborhood filled the windows, the balustrades that curled elegant as clefs, and he took my hand and kissed it, telling me he could always hope I'd change my mind.

This was something my mother had often said, sweetly, in the face of a circumstance she couldn't fix and that made me unhappy. A pluck to her posture, a camp to her smile, her brown back teeth not yet crumbled and pulled. *Give it five hot minutes, and you might change your mind.*

REPUTATION MANAGEMENT

◆

Alice Niemand had been working for the company two years when the young Hasidic man died, and it made her look at her things, the cashmere cardigans and the pebbled bath mats, and consider how she had earned the money to buy them. On a normal day, it was easy enough not to examine: she never went into a workplace, never talked to anyone who did the same job she did, never discussed aloud the clients whose reputations she had repaired. She never shook their hands or heard their voices, these lawyers and dentists, PTA mothers with some angry review or mug shot to suppress. The boy who was dead, freshly nineteen, had been the victim of sexual abuse by the Yeshiva teacher whose reputation Alice repaired. He had *claimed* to be his victim, she reminded herself, but then came another feeling, lower in her body, which seemed to ask, in the way it roiled: why would anyone claim that?

On the coast of California where the garnet had eroded to make the sand purple, and from a multicolored veranda in the New Orleans garden district, and in view of children pushing toy boats in the Jardin du Luxembourg, she had reviewed files summarizing lives and careers and misdemeanors, had typed the stiff sentences that financed her comfortable life. Her parents were as impressed by her new place in the world as they were intimidated by the gifts she sent to their sagging split-level home in the middle of the country. What could they do with an iPad that they couldn't on their computer, the pauses between their thank-yous said, what should they put on these asymmetrical walnut serving boards? Would she be visiting sometime? They were sorry to say they did not have the money to make it to New York. It was never mentioned that the cost of the things Alice sent easily exceeded a couple round-way tickets.

Alice had bumped from one Craigslist apartment to the next in the years after college, making friends chiefly to learn from them, when to tilt the head in the course of flirtation, how to conduct oneself in an expensive restaurant, never telling anyone about her father's job ringing up purchases of gas and Snickers, her mother's meager income selling Mary Kay cosmetics. She had visited the office, a hyper-color portrait of Silicon Valley opulence, for three interviews and a training session. It was 2012, her last month in San Francisco, and the last quarter in which the company bothered to meet any freelancer in person.

A guy on a skateboard had careened down an aisle that separated two rows of desks, clipping the heels of the formal, uncomfortable shoes Alice wore, and she watched as he landed on an L-shaped couch and began to comment on a foosball game. To the right of a freestanding iron staircase nearby, a man jogging on a treadmill typed on a computer that hovered above it. "Casey prefers the running desk to the standing," Alice's tour guide explained, with a satisfied laugh that she understood she was meant to mimic. In the company kitchen, the snack foods, arranged by color, sat up straight on transparent shelving. "There is such a thing," she heard a departing tour leader say to a group of new IT personnel, "as a free lunch."

All this forced irreverence aside, the company, it was quick to assert to the new writers in the all-glass conference room that day, had principles. They did not work with felons, or people found guilty of domestic abuse, or convicted sex offenders. Standing in front of a whiteboard, a tanned man in thin designer cotton spoke to Alice's group with the wry twist of his mouth, his California upbringing apparent in every protracted syllable. "These people in general are, like, not dudes you want to be having dinner with. The good news, right, is you don't have to. Our sales reps take care of that." A titter unfolded in the room and the new hires leaned back in the ergonomic chairs. "You just deal with their files." Ethan resembled some beautiful, off-limits older brother, tall and freckled, blessed with the demeanor of those who always seem just-roused from some luxurious sleep. In the afternoons, a dripping wetsuit could be seen hanging in his office. As he coached her on her first customer, Ethan brushed a light hand on her elbow. Together they giggled about the client's sham company, which sold advertising space on magnets with the false promise of distribution in small towns. Cackling at its website's "About Us" section, filled with dated stock photos of big-haired women before enormous computers—"Who could fall for this?" he had laughed—Ethan shot her a glance of unmetered approval. "You're doing such a great job, by the way. It's a little scary how fast you learn." She was, she marveled, mastering it quickly: all she had to do was write three hundred words, essays in miniature, that made her clients seem more impressive and decent than they were. By the surveys the customers filled out, Alice could immediately identify the people they saw themselves as being, and then she wrote that person into existence, her voice transforming accordingly. A person who listed scuba diving as a hobby was always *an adventurer as well as a professional*, and the individual who wrote "books, especially Mystries and Crime" *an avid intellectual.* She padded the pieces with SEO tags and handed them over to the web team, who situated links in places unknown to her, ultimately pushing the clients' embarrassing or disturbing Google search results to page five or six. Gone were the variously threatening and pitiful voicemails they had left for their exes, gone the lawsuits involving unpaid child support.

There is no direct interfacing with the clients, Alice would say later, a thoughtful index finger on her cheek, when people asked about her job. This was the phrase she'd been taught to use.

In the beginning, when the nature of the work was still novel, Alice had googled each case assigned to her, read the drunk-in-public arrest report, the vicious *Gawker* article about the tantrum, or the affair with an intern. A few direct deposit paychecks later she ceased to do this, as it only added time to each job and diverted her thoughts as she tried to write the glib summaries of careers and personal achievements. *Dedicated equally to his family and to his career*, she would write, the dry introductory clauses coming to her automatically, *so-and-so enjoys yachting with his two sons and traveling with his wife*. After six months on the job, she could handle three cases each day, which roughly amounted to $77,000 a year, a figure that would have seemed improbable to her beforehand. *One of the most admired minds in the world of litigation*, she would write. *Alan Nixon remains a dental health professional committed to both furthering his education and supporting his community*. The balances on her student loans were vanishing, the recurrent nightmares of creditors gone from her sleep. It was the first time in her adult life that her talents as a chameleon had felt translatable, and also that she hadn't smelled of the entrées carried three at a time on her forearm.

The Yeshiva teacher's file had not given her much to begin with. She got those, sometimes, people who—despite having paid thousands of dollars for the service—could not be bothered to fill out the forms about their career, their hobbies, their philanthropic endowments. They provided only a birthday, a name. Dov Abraham supplied only the Yeshiva and its address. The anonymous supervisor she chatted with—the company had transferred Ethan, done away with traditional models of management, at least with regard to the freelance writers—advised Alice to write about the client's place of work. This meant producing a great deal of filler and jamming his name into every other sentence, no matter the lingual acrobatics required. *Dedicated to its students and the greater community alike, the Viznitz Yeshiva for Boys organizes numerous events, the majority overseen by Dov Abraham, which enrich and educate. The Viznitz Yeshiva for Boys and Dov Abraham are known in the surrounding neighborhood as bastions of Hasidic culture and faith.*

After she read about the suicide in the paper, she could not help arranging the facts of it in the hyperbolic, humorless tone of the pieces she wrote for the company. *A pedophile for more than twenty-five years,* she thought, *Dov Abraham takes intrepid measures to prevent any members of his community from exposing him.* It was her mind's way of inflicting punishment, keeping her from any moment of relief.

On a date with a man who asked the waitress too many questions about the wine, was it effervescent, was it biodynamic, she continued to compose. *Particularly passionate about shy children, Dov Abraham first poses as a mentor to gain the trust of their families.* "A Sancerre sounds perfect," she said. The rest of the evening felt like following another car, changing lanes and matching turn signals but grasping nothing of the route itself. Her date was making a case for children's access to social media. He was talking about the shift in American philanthropic giving patterns, or about the term *post-racial*, or about his family's summer home.

Although she could not remember much of what was said over dinner, or perhaps because of the guilt she felt about this, Alice agreed to a taxi back to his apartment and the sexual contract that entailed. It was the only respite she'd found from her obsession with the story, on her knees with her forearms flexed and hips raised as he moved behind her. These were the only minutes in which her thoughts slackened, and as she came, bucking him backward, unrelated memories presented themselves in blithe procession: a Mexican bakery's lights going on in the very early morning, a cat strolling through a damp Louisiana cemetery, rinsed grains and washed spinach near an open window. He may as well have been faceless, but still she ran a hand across his collarbone, after, and spent six naked, unconscious hours in his company.

On the train home she felt ashamed in front of the commuters, who stood there with admirable posture, just-groomed and well-prepared for the work ahead of them. She hid behind her honey sunglasses, acutely aware of her own smell, the wine she hadn't brushed from her teeth, the sex she hadn't showered off. *Dov Abraham employs numerous methods when manipulating a minor, including chaperoned trips to traditional bathhouses and one-on-one tutoring sessions.* In the last six months, the company had let go the majority of the writers and re-hired new, outsourced talent under the guise of a different, nebulous group called AirCommunications. Her survival was the result of an exacting exam on company grammar and style, meant to weed out all but the unassailable among the writers. She had always enjoyed the space of a test, the clarity of the task, the time alone with her flexed and ready mind, and she had been among the few who passed.

Back in her apartment, she boiled water and ground coffee and set the stewing titanium French press near her laptop. By her standards, she was late to log in to the SharedWorkspace, but there was no one appointed to notice; time existed only vis-à-vis the proof it had been filled. AirCommunications required she enable a productivity-monitoring app once she began writing, but until then her actions were not tracked. Unable to click on the queue of tasks that had filtered in overnight, paralyzed by the sentences her guilt continued to write, she opened a window to compose an email to Ethan. Though he had long since stopped working as the writers' supervisor, he favored her and occasionally sent her special assignments. She still had his address with his real name attached, a piece of information he asked her never to share. Everyone else in AirCommunications' SharedWorkspace knew him as Anakin, a research and development expert who occasionally surfaced to lead digital seminars.

From: AliceN@aircomm.com

To: EthanT@reputationprotection.com

Date: March 7, 2014 at 11:22 a.m. EST

Subject: client screening

Hi Ethan—

Long time, pal. How is everything in your new position? I miss you in "The Writer's Room."

Anyway, I'm writing for a slightly odd reason. A few months ago I had this client, Dov Abraham. He hadn't been convicted of anything, but last week this nineteen-year-old kid, who claimed to have been sexually abused by Abraham, jumped off a bridge. I'm wondering if we can use this to start a conversation about company policy—maybe the rule about no convictions is not filter enough? Could we woodshed on a different type of screening? Given that you're higher up and I'm just a freelancer, I thought going to you might be the right first step. What do you think?

All my best,
Alice

From: EthanT@reputationprotection.com
To: AliceN@aircomm.com
Date: March 7, 2014 at 11:57 a.m EST
Subject: re: client screening

Hey Alice!

Long time, dude. Hope you're doing well out there in New York!

Wow, that is a real bummer to read and I hear you 110 percent about how conflicted you must be feeling. I looked into the case and it seems like the sales reps did some pretty heavy vetting and just could not have predicted this, you know? He appeared to be someone very invested in his community who truly needed our product to repair his reputation, and because he was never even tried we had to assume he had been wronged. Unfortunately I can't help you out with moving this up bc I'm working in ideation now and don't even have contact with that branch. Just remember you are a super talented writer and this company has really benefited from your hard work. :)

Cheers!
Ethan

Alice read and reread the email, looking each time for the encouraging support or helpful directive she knew it did not contain. Then she went back to the article about the boy who was gone. Looking at the news was a kind of psychedelic doom—new facts brought into the existing article, under the same headline, as though they had been there all along, and it was you, in your ignorance, who had failed to absorb them. What she believed were the new sentences stood out and waved to her, taunting her with a deepening sense of tragedy. The *Times* had expanded the paragraph about the traditional bathhouse, where the teacher had frequently taken the boy, to include the name and location. Now the piece closed with an anecdote from that morning, in which a group of men had surrounded Abraham as he left his home, shielding him from the small cluster of protesters as he made his way to work. The series of related photos had also multiplied, though the composition of most was similar—the silhouette of the same hat, the same box-shouldered coat, repeated, a crowd of men with their heads down and an army of hands raised to block the camera's view. There remained just one photo of the boy, taken before the community had shunned him. He still wore the curls around his face, the yarmulke, the starched shirt: his face made a decent impression of a teenager's, but the tone of his skin was blanched, the way he buttoned his lips an indication of adult worries. He had left Williamsburg shortly after he turned eighteen, ostensibly hoping that the scandal of his accusations would die down, that his parents and six siblings could resume their regular lives, that the low anonymous voices would stop calling, that the notes taped to their windows every morning would cease to appear. In the year following his disappearance from the community, he had washed dishes at an Olive Garden in Times Square, showed up early for every shift. He had also arrived with time to spare for his own suicide, strolled the Manhattan bridge for a full hour in the February dark before going over.

Alice had failed to attach to the idea of a god, to the culture of a family, but she was envious of anyone who could. That the boy had been pushed from the comforts of his faith and his household was with Alice as she wrote her first public post.

CommunityBoard: AirCommunications
Subj: Re-evaluating Our Standards

Author: AliceN
12:06:54 p.m. EST

Hi writers and editors:

Many of you may recall working on pieces for Dov Abraham, who purchased a package of 40 bios. Recently, a young man from Abraham's Orthodox community in Brooklyn, NY, took his own life after his accusations of sexual abuse by Abraham resulted in threats to him and his family. Abraham was never charged and thus screened as an approved client. I feel that something should change about the way we filter customers, and I wonder if we might all put our heads together and discuss a solution. Thanks in advance for putting some time towards this important issue.

All my best,
Alice N

CommunityBoard: AirCommunications
Re: Re-evaluating Our Standards
Author: EliseR
12:13:12 p.m. EST

That is so sad. I have been working as a writer for six months and have wondered the same thing on a couple occasions—could the company maybe turn down people with pending accusations against them, or implement a waiting period to see whether the accusations have been substantiated?

CommunityBoard: AirCommunications
Re: Re-evaluating Our Standards

Author: Supervisor

12:16:32 p.m EST

Thanks for your input, team. At AirCommunications we truly value your insight and discerning judgment. Our customer service department does everything possible to screen our clientele, and will continue to do so.

12:16:46 p.m. EST

This post has been closed to further comments by Supervisor.

The post was shut down in under ten minutes, deleted in thirteen. She had watched it happen like a member of any audience, a viewer at home helpless to the outcome, someone who would later decide the ending had been inevitable. Soon another post appeared in the CommunityBoard, reminders about style and grammar, and banal responses and subresponses filtered in by the handful. *When it comes to parallelism*, someone wrote. Alice closed her computer and crawled onto her made bed, the well-matched lilacs and grays, and she slept off most of the afternoon, the hand-tooled leather belt she wore around her waist pressing a welt there.

She opened her computer once more that evening, in the depressive haze that followed her nap, the screen the only source of light in her darkened bedroom. Nobody had emailed her directly, though a post about SharedWorkspace etiquette did appear, and she scanned the veiled sentences for a clear judgment of her behavior. . . . *Given the sensitive nature of our work ... clientele privacy is of utmost concern ... extensively trained sales representatives ...* Alice was back asleep in under an hour, and she dreamt of a nagging electronic buzz coming from a device she couldn't find and didn't know she owned.

She did not have the chance to make the decision for herself. When she logged in the next day, partially out of habit and partially because she wanted to escort her anger somewhere relevant, she found no new posts, no tasks waiting in her queue. She refreshed it every few minutes for most of an hour, checking the news and social media in other tabs, feeling increasingly that each shallow breath she took was an effort pulled off at the last minute. Her apartment around her remained as comforting as she had made it—the low periwinkle couch with splayed wooden legs and the spotless sheepskin beneath it, the spider plant she had trained to grow down an antique ladder—and she had never hated a place more, never wanted to leave as badly. She packed a bag with a panicked assortment of things, some face wipes and an extra sweater and a packet of dried apricots, and at the last minute she removed her phone and left it on the granite kitchen counter. She was not going anywhere in particular, and she would not need any directions to get there. There was nothing it could tell her, Alice thought, no email or text or weather alert or Tinder match, that would change how she felt.

Before she even stepped into the train, she realized what she had told herself, that she had nowhere in mind, was not true. She knew first by which direction she chose, then by which line, then by the way she settled into her seat to wait out the long ride. She was sure when she emerged into the gray world and saw the families, the men dressed like all the other men and the women like all the other women, moving in united huddles down the sidewalks. She knew by the sound of the muttered Yiddish, by the sudden and foreign envy she felt for the wigs the women wore, those automatic signifiers of purity. They were probably not the women who had feigned ignorance when they heard what the boy said was done to his body, Alice told herself, the men who had surrounded Abraham to shield him from the press.

March in New York was confused—a bleached blue sky, a corrosive wind—and it felt to her not like a certain season but the weather's selfish refusal to decide on one. She skulked behind the families, made itchy by the thought that they had known the boy, spoken or refused to speak about him over the warmth of their crowded dinner tables. As she cut up to their side, they grouped automatically to the right or left, avoiding her as they would some broken glass. When she was past them she hurried along, feeling very much the foreigner she was there, her hair tangled and too long, her clothing of too many colors. In her town there had been Christmas pageants at her parents' Lutheran church, pancake feeds to support the fire department each fall, spring carnivals where one-hit wonders performed to a slumped drunk audience, but these had been traditions that asked nothing of her. She had slipped out of that place as easily as a hand from a pocket. Her mother and father had been the only family she'd known, and they, too, had required little of Alice, had failed to create some orienting bond, even a few private jokes that could be leaned on when necessary. In the eight years since she'd left home, her father had become one of those people who lurked around ancestry. com, and sometimes, without any attached commentary, he sent her links to a patch of people he suspected were their relatives, a bread maker named Flossie or a Civil War veteran and his twin boys who had died of typhus. Clicking around there inspired very little in her, felt about as personal as a trip to the DMV, and because she could not determine the correct reply to these emails she did not respond at all.

The image of her parents, silent before their television without a word or a look for the other, seemed to flash at her back as she passed up the street. She wanted now to be unimpeded, she needed to walk alone and quickly. As soon as she was past one family, she was upon another, all of them unbothered by the vicious gusting, caught up in a conversation that had gone on for happy years. They were coming and going from every direction, milling through the iron gates of houses with plastic awnings, filling the crosswalks, their hands linked, their skin moon-pale and immaculate. She wanted to visit the places that had made up the boy's life, the synagogue where he'd been quiet and the park where he'd been loud, but she had no internal map of the city where she lived, had never bothered to develop one. Alice put a question about a street to a young mother of twins, but she produced no more than a vague southern wave before she hurried away.

A half an hour later, Alice was down by the water. The scent of the East River was never restorative—it smelled more like something fermenting, turning over and over in the sweat of not getting anywhere. Still, it was better to be sitting on this bench, in view of the rotting, mossy piles, than weaving through the mass of people who belonged to each other. She had found a relatively quiet place to consider where she would go next in order to not go home, and she was alone save the presence of a man a few years younger. He stood six feet behind her, blowing on his bare hands, pulling a sheepskin collar closer to his neck, scrutinizing his phone and the water in equal measure. Her fingers had just begun to slacken, and her jaw had just let up its working, when the hat came into view.

It was the shape from all the news photos, the wide brim and the severe line of the top, and for a moment it was an inch from her toes. She expected the owner to follow, but he didn't, and then she saw a gust filling the hat again, lifting one side of it. Alice had dressed badly, in layers that failed to keep the wind out, and she felt a certain satisfaction watching it, this thing also the victim of bad weather. Did she want the wind to die down, to let it rest, or to animate it more fully, bring it across the rocks and into the river? Alice let the thought go: her attention was divided now between the wobble of the flapping felt and the approaching sound of labored breathing. The man was running in shallow steps, holding his coat closed, obviously pained by the exposure of his hair and scalp, his *payots* oscillating, still too far from the hat to save it from its path toward the water. The birthmark on his face was the red of strawberry juice. Alice gave him a mollifying flash of her palm, and she reached down and pinched.

When she rose she was aware of an internal pressure and warmth, something like one might feel when passing over an earnestly considered, long-planned and saved-for gift. She wanted to smile and hand the man this thing he needed, wanted to communicate that it had been no problem to help him in this way. She wanted to say that the silk lining was lovely, that she could appreciate the craftsmanship. But she also needed him to nod and thank her, which she soon saw he could and would not. He was fixated on the hat in her hands, his eyes not moving from where her fingers held it. When she extended it toward him his hands flew up and his knees bent, and they did this several times, his dip becoming deeper in each frantic iteration. Her thoughts moved from disappointment to anger in a matter of seconds, and it did not feel like a choice, then, when she spoke.

"Oh, you can't take it because I've touched it? You think I've poisoned the hat?" She knew, in fact, what his upbringing had told him not to do, which was to let his fingers meet hers, but she did not release her grip. She brought the hat to her chest, making it impossible for him to touch it without touching her.

He was leaning incrementally backward with his hands spread, sweat pearling on his bare forehead, looking like something hunted.

"What is it you think I've done to it? You ran after it but you won't take it?" She kept rocking onto her front foot, bending then straightening her arm to offer then withdraw the hat. "I'm so impure that you can't accept something I've saved for you? It would be better if it had flown into the East River? I'm so evil that I don't count as human? I'm Alice Niemand, and I saved this fucking hat because I thought it would matter to you." She had never heard vitriol in her own voice, never issued anything close to a speech, never admitted to hate.

When she finally threw it—onto a strip of yellow grass, still patched with the last snow—behind him, when she watched him whirl around, she felt a schism in her body, a divorce of her anger from the rest of her. The rotten part that had blistered was still there, but now it was observable, open to her own judgment. She did not notice the man who had lingered and watched them, his face made joyful by the phone he held to it. Her shame and shock carried her forward, up some blocks into a more trafficked area, where she poured herself into a cab.

At home, in the queen-sized bed whose softness felt undeserved, she saw herself on loop, taunting the man, ridiculing the only beliefs he knew, pitching the hat. She paused the memory to rehash his reaction, how her cruelty had hit his face, how he had eaten at his bottom lip and not known where to look. She saw the birthmark intensifying in color. She ran circles around these details until finally an overheated sleep came, and it kept her eleven hours, through the sun's decline and return.

When Alice woke, she could not remember the routine she

was meant to follow, was unsure what the necessary steps for reacquainting herself with the world might be—did she need food, or a shower, or an in-person conversation with someone who claimed to know her? When she groped for her phone to check the time she saw a text from her last one-night stand. It was rare she reached out to these people and rarer she heard from them.

Personally, I think you look hot with those horns. You're famous, Alice Niemand!

She began her reply— *Which horns do you*—but as she did another part of her had already begun to answer the question. Alice typed her name into the search bar, she clicked the link, she watched the video.

Acquaintances who used the app had demonstrated it for her: it was always goofy, the mutual distortion of features a proof of bonding. Get close together! Add the nose of a pig! Swap your friend's teeth and eyes for your own! Affix a clown's bow tie, stamp the text of an exclusive joke, show the world your boundless, flexible, fun-loving self. Send it direct or make it public, make it evidence of your multicolored, multipeopled, widely envied life. She had never considered it could be used this way, the mockery as vicious as the silliness was vital.

I AM ALICE NIEMAND!!!! said a pulsing banner of text, red then black then red. Over and over, her mouth unleashing the forked tongue of a snake. Her hand making a *thwong* every time she holds out the hat. The recursive sprouting of sallow horns from her head. The audio was incomplete but unaltered, *I am Alice Niemand and I saved this fucking hat, I am Alice Niemand*

and I saved this fucking hat. 8,567,122 views. *HOT BIGOT LOSES HER MIND.* Even she could see that the filters were so effective for how well they matched her as she truly was in that moment, the voice in a register that belonged to the deranged and schizophrenic, the glare unconcerned with the society on the periphery.

———

The email came a week later. She had not worked, and had no plans to work; she had not left, and had no desire to leave. Alice Niemand lay circumscribed by single socks, moisturizers, ossified tissues, spent jars of peanut butter, books begun and abandoned, blouses retrieved from the closet but never slipped on. When she tugged down the screen of her phone for the thousandth, passive time, as she lay in the foul, clotted smell of her bedsheets, the vibration of Ethan's email made her sit up.

From: EthanT@reputationprotection.com

To: Alice.Niemand@gmail.com

Date: March 20, 2014 at 1:07 p.m. EST

Hey Alice!

Hope it's ok to write you over here on your personal email. I know that your queue has not been getting any tasks lately and I was wondering whether you had any interest in a special project! It's for a friend of mine and I know he needs a really focused creative person who can write circles around the rest of us so I thought of you OF COURSE!

Basically the deal is he's starting a new pharma-tech-pub company—there's a lot of VC excitement over here in CA, and it seems like it's really gonna take off. But he needs writers to really make it sing. The idea is you would write reports and reviews about new prescriptions, pulling from studies and testimonials the pharma company has provided you, to be positioned all over the place. Rate is def. competitive. Let me know if this sounds good and I'll put you in touch!

Thanks dude!
Ethan

Alice swung her legs over the edge of the bed and curled her toes in the rug that lay clean on the floor. She was composing a reply in her head, striking the right tone—confident, grateful, capable—when her phone hummed with a bright note. In a manic fit the night prior, she had told herself that enough was enough, that she would no longer allow herself to fester, and ordered the things that would make her life recognizable to her. Now they had arrived in her foyer, the fresh produce and the lauded memoir and the sulfate-free shampoo, and they would keep her fed and clean for days. In the elevator down, she admired the light as it moved to illuminate each button, the cheerful two-part sound that meant arrival on the lowest floor. She had heard a great deal about the evils of modern technology, how its solutions were too focused on the individual, but Alice, for one, felt thankful for a world that let her stay exactly where she needed to be.

TEMPORARY HOUSING

♦

Only Greg ever noticed the notch in my tooth, and only in outline did I tell him about how I got it, how Guin and I had stolen that couple's developed film from the "J" cubby in the Tuttle Drug. Tall and poor, she and I had walked through downtown Petaluma in each other's clothing, our pupils dilated by one drug or shrunk by another. People thought we were fucking, or whatever mean verb they'd use to describe what bodies like ours could do with another, but the closest we came was sleeping naked. The closest we came was dreaming some vague man on top, and waking confused to the sight of a real, new woman. If asked to explain the end of that friendship, I might still blame the night we ruined that marriage. It's easier to claim there was one bad day, a cheap little kindness you can spend against the debt of one bad life.

Guin was originally from Utah, a daughter who'd been spanked to welts for swearing against Jesus too often, asking about the looks her family had started to get at church, but I'd been punished more by chance, and silence. Little-girl dinners I had to fix myself in the pantry, saltines and brown apples, on evenings my parents wouldn't emerge after a fight. That Guin and I were poor, or unhappy, for different reasons—my parents boomer dropouts who came from middle-class security but destroyed their own chance of it, her mother a missionary never given a thing—didn't register in the aisles of the Grocery Outlet where our families both shopped. During those years I'd all but dropped out, becoming the gossiped-about mystery of the honors class girls who had been my friends, our miseries seemed to correspond exactly. I convinced myself soon after this was something closer to a coincidence, a tacky suitcase you find at a flea market that happens to bear your own monogrammed initials. You register the fact and move on, a little embarrassed that a part of you could be so recognizable, and reproducible.

"You are unwell," a client snaps at me, on what is something like a Tuesday afternoon, something like eight months into the virus. She's angry about my suggestion—an anti-psychotic, Latuda, for a pattern of intrusive thoughts about killing her husband—and that I've seemed tired, and elsewhere. "Have you even been listening to the complexity of this, or are you just another pusher? That's what my fucking schizophrenic uncle takes, and I'm not a schizophrenic. I'm a *good* mother and a *successful* entrepreneur."

"I'm sorry," I say, and roll my chair a little toward the screen to let her know I'm listening. "I hear that you're feeling misunderstood."

The client's thoughts have become the defining feature of all our recent sessions—how they intrude as she watches her husband take the bottles of formula from the fridge, or teach the five-year-old about the lawn mower by giving its different parts funny voices. A screwdriver in the neck! A gas leak while she's out! They flash to her mind like things that have already happened, and can't be helped.

"How could I be running an award-winning *yarn store*," she says, "if I were some dangerous lunatic?" That line I would have repeated to Greg, and it would have fed us for months. *Actually, rather easily*, he would have retorted in apostrophe, his handsome face smiling in a way that tripled my devotion in a second, *and maybe with a few tax deductions*. "Also," she says, "I *hate* that thing you do with your tongue." I start to apologize: it's just a habit of thoughtfulness, how I must push it visibly against my teeth, but she closes her laptop and shuts me back into my life.

Maybe two hours later, as I take in the pond from our Palladian window—its placement under the side gable is unusual for a Federal house—my phone lights up, a spam call with my hometown area code. Social Security number soon to be erased, a voice says, due to illicit possession. It's a good trick, on their part. They must bet on how many Americans might like it, the opportunity to pick up a familiar number, if only for the turn to say, *No!*, if only for the chance to say, *No longer!*

———

Guin and I were waiting, that day, on a roll I'd taken of a dreaming, episodic acid trip: mostly of her, a few with the twenty-eight-year-old speed freak she was dating. We took turns slamming our palms flat on the bell until the balding, name-tagged Kenneth appeared from behind the curtain already tired of us. He absorbed our complaint and disappeared again. We started rifling at opposite ends of the alphabet, bored with the same old photos of our shiny lip-glossed enemies—posing on Jettas in stretch denim, glittery thongs apparent, or holding each other in mirrors bombed by a disposable's flash—and met in the middle. I found the envelope, but Guin snatched it from my hands.

A childless couple in their early thirties, the Joneses' life was one I had never given a swirling thought. They lived near me, five blocks uphill, far from the sounds of the boulevard's traffic that filled my mother's apartment. He taught sixth grade and choir at a grammar school—unhappily, it was known, and pedantically—and she designed websites for people in cities. I'd only ever noticed the dog they followed in and out of their Queen Anne, a saluki whose elegance seemed gaudy in that town of hokey editorials and ripped, bored cops. I loved Petaluma, even as I looked forward to leaving, and felt a real pride in where I was from, maybe trained by my father who had adored it, always honking when crossing back into city limits.

You could see the Jones dog outside the café where they stopped mornings for espresso, sitting silent and certain. It would not move its shiny head for the passerby who tried to pet it, not even gentle pats of children, nor would it bark. *What are you*, Guin said to it once, when she tried to touch it, *some celebrity on his day off?* That couple were part of a wave of others like them, leaving San Francisco after the tech bubble burst. They were the same people who would make it so eventually the docks had gated fences, and the smarter restaurants took down their folksy, loving signs—one day they were pleased to serve you, the next they knew the pleasure had better be yours.

The first photos focused on their house's restoration, mid-morning singing through the refurbished glass portico, molded cherubs at high corners. I wasn't as compelled by it all as Guin. The subtleties of money, how it could be spent, didn't interest me yet, perhaps because my father had been fixated on a lack of it. He was two years sober when he received his larceny sentence. A winsome barber with sixty college credits in philosophy, he'd run a scam he claimed to believe only hurt the credit card companies, not the customers he charged three times. The summer before I left town, my mother was already doing her own Sisyphean time, paying off the high-interest debt she'd run up the first fall he was gone. There'd been nothing enormous: acrylic turtlenecks, a refurbished off-brand laptop for each of us. She ultimately declared bankruptcy, but in those years she was still trying to make it right, buying drugstore-brand stockings for her job as a law firm secretary.

Soon they were going to change her position from contractor to employee, she would assure me, though I hadn't asked. I didn't need a doctor, and didn't notice she couldn't go to one. Clothes and books covered the bed she hadn't made since my father left it, asking the same question her face did while she smoked. What was the lesson, could anyone say? For which occasion was she supposed to dress? It must have seemed to her that the moment she stopped picking him off the couch where he'd passed out drunk, he stood up quietly to become a thief.

Guin glanced through the snapshots with her eyes half-raised, awaiting the moment the clerk would return. Here was the brass finial, rising above repainted lilacs and blues. Next came a day at Dillon Beach, Mrs. Jones disappearing behind mounds of sand in jewel-toned leggings, then the two of them in matching Cal baseball caps. The shining, prissy dog leaping. As we came upon the image of her twined to the bed frame with luminous black cords, her face lifted in devotion, the clerk reappeared.

I kept his eye and nodded as he rang us up, knowing as I did that Guin had slipped the envelope down the back of her jeans. Guin put her hand in mine and thanked him so politely—*Gee, I super-appreciate it, Kenny*—he frowned in suspicion. Guin's occasional manners were a vestige of a Mormon childhood, a way of life killed as suddenly as her father was: his own gun, the garage, eleven in the morning. Guin had been eight, and lied to about the nature of his death, but she'd figured it out by the time she was twelve and they'd moved to California. A dyslexic who never spelled a word the same way twice, she was eighteen that summer, and had earned her GED two years before. After I stopped showing up to class, I had graduated, barely, through some independent study loophole granted to those with "trouble at home." If we were free then, it was a peculiar kind of freedom—both the kind of daughters who needed to spy, we treated our own lives like something to be infiltrated, armed and blazing.

The June morning was warm, but not severe, as we left the drugstore and crossed the bridge toward the old mill. Its steel coruscated above the remains of the railroad, which had once carried eggs from the town's farmers to San Francisco. It now stood rotting over the fetid estuary—slow, brown water the town always called "the river." Back at my mother's apartment, a flat sectioned from what had once been a single-family Stick Victorian, we took off our shirts and settled on the concrete back patio. It was almost pleasant there, with a row of plants in terra-cotta plastic, and an assortment of mildly broken furniture. A wobbly glass table, an umbrella sprouting from the center at a crooked angle. Two wooden chaise lounges that could no longer be adjusted, their hardware rusted from winter rain. The only object that worked as it should was the ashtray, a metal contraption that spun and lowered, when pressed, to conceal the butts in its belly. Guin loved that thing, and called it the Forgetter.

Memories, the drugstore packages said, in a bendy font that faded in thickness, toward the word's conclusion, to become confetti. On the table between us Guin placed the image where we'd stopped before. The woman lay on her stomach, her wrists bound together behind her back, her legs kept in a V by the cords that secure her ankles to either end of the footboard. Her turned face on the pillow, canted slightly up, doesn't look at the camera. As for the gag in her mouth, it seems like something that was always there.

Sick, Guin said, as she flipped to the next photo, where he appeared alongside her in the mirror—one arm crossing her torso like a seat belt to choke her, and the other holding up a whip. Guin brought that print closer to look at the leather cord, trying to get a real sense of its harm. *I can't look anymore*, she said, after scouring all of them twice. *We should do something about this.*

When I asked why she was so pissed about some boring softcore, she snapped at me that *anyone could have seen these, what he's doing to her.* If she believed her reaction to be on behalf of Mrs. Jones, I only felt a sad jolt of confirmation. Even if I couldn't say it yet, I must have suspected the point of my body was its capture. Which little girl, fed those shiny Disney VHSes, could avoid the suggestion? That *her* equivalent of the western, the movies her father loved—those open, lawless spaces, the galloping speed—would come in the shape of one person, a boy who came along if you did your good waiting.

Guin sat there fuming, smoke pouring from her mouth toward the sun, but I was as calm as I always managed to be during that spell of my life. Like many children of alcoholics, I could read faces very well—as a psychiatrist, it's helped me—and so those photos didn't alarm me. Anger or fear, love or hatred: those feelings seemed as absent from that bedroom as any other clutter, silenced by the dahlias on the end table, or folded neatly within the lilac throw. I didn't much see the point in looking for them. But then I've always liked explaining people's lives a little too neatly, or that's what Greg thought, saying that was why I got into my line of work.

This isn't real violence, I said. Guin looked at me then the way someone does when you brightly call them the incorrect name, long after you ought to have known it—hurt enough, by a mistake so crucial, that a correction hardly feels worth the breath.

I went inside to piss, and as I flushed I heard Guin call she was leaving, a nasty slam of the gate. These sorts of exits were occurring more often, likely in reaction to mine, which was impending. In the fall I'd applied to college—drunk, online, and barely, receiving no acceptances but one waitlist from a mediocre private school I knew little about—and when the letter came, I made the mistake of showing Guin my excitement. The brochure of hideous, brand-new buildings, the palm trees that screamed useless, lifelong debt. *It looks like a bad mall where you can't even shop*, she said, a line I would use as my own to people in my classes. By then Guin and I weren't speaking.

———————

That remark about my job: I think Greg made it the first year in Vermont, when we were thirty and mostly happy, chatting with people in the co-op about novels and politics. He taught rich kids classics over at Deerfield, just over the Massachusetts border, and liked chiding them in Greek about ancient questions, being addressed as *Doctor* during coat-and-tie lunches. As for me, as the small-town shrink, I felt I was something like the masonry downtown—designed to protect people, but safe from being changed much by their lives. I loved all the granite in Brattleboro, the quartzite of the Gothic church sourced on Wantastiquet Mountain. That kind of architecture is hard to find in this country, where we were in such a hurry to get started that chopping down a tree made more sense than finding and quarrying the right kind of stone. I felt as devoted to Vermont as I did to Greg, loved its order and drama of time.

That the leaves in October were as saffron as the snow would be white, that the mating bullfrogs in spring were as loud as the winter mountains had been silent. In Northern California you get from primeval redwoods to sun-painted ocean in a half hour flat, piney peaks to tawny pasture without stopping for lunch. Sometimes I want to blame what Greg called my lost years on that landscape. Of course it was my father, of course it was my mother, but wasn't it also that a day could feel like a year, that the scope of what you saw could explode one minute and shrink the next? Who knew what you were reacting to, the earth that didn't need you or your life that only might? How could you trust any feeling? To my father, a southerner who still called the ocean *the sea*, that climate was thrilling. He had loved small talk about weather as much as the weather itself.

My family was very different from Guin's, but there *was* one strange coincidence between us, I guess I forgot to say—both of our fathers had killed themselves. He'd *told* my mother he couldn't do prison, she would repeat in the months after the call came from the DOC. And as with many things—how to swim under a nasty wave, how to hike down a steep hill and keep your balance—he had been right.

The Joneses' photos, I thought, couldn't have shocked Guin as much as she pretended: we had learned hooks and jabs from a video we paused and replayed on my boxy laptop, and our party trick—she was more convincing—was to make the teenage Spencers and Brians we knew, sweatshirted creatures with bongwater eyes, bleed from their noses, without warning or reason. Local boys were friends, but little else—we had fake IDs used for nights in the city that felt like whole futures, and required something like investigative journalism to piece together later. Oblivion or velocity, Guin had her preferences—already loyal to downers, she occasionally needed some all-night chatter—but I could do one or the other as if it were an aimless matter of left or right. For her birthday in the spring, we had gobbled Vicodin and sucked lollipops on the 80 into the city, playing up the irony that we might be girls who loved sugar, waving at sweet old women and calling them ma'am. I loved how an opiate made you aware of your lungs, the shallow breathing that courted those enormous sighs. At the Steinhardt Aquarium, yet to be remodeled, redolent still with salt water leaking onto carpet, our breathing felt religious. We worshipped before enormous turtles who had lived forever, the shifting walls of fish whose only job was to be a certain color, and float toward the edges of their life. *Oh, I love that ole dang squid*, Guin said, kissing the glass, swiveling around to kiss me. Those drugs made her enchanted with everything and everyone—on our way in, she had gasped at the blue eyes of an elderly security guard and said, *Sir, are you aware you're my husband?*—but I took what I could get.

On nights there was blow or Dexedrine glowing through our pockets, the goal was a room that looked like nowhere with a door closed to everything, paid for often with the tips we both made busing tables. When we had less money there were men in tourist neighborhoods, harmless commuters or Cal State bros, who could be convinced to come along to whichever motel and pitch in. Greg would have been upset if

I told him that part, or thought it was something like prostitution. There are so many nice, half-safe places on the way to getting rid of yourself, I wouldn't have been able to convince him, decent people who only give you what you've persuaded them you need.

So much I didn't say, and still he was the rare person who knew much about that part of my life—only because I had to explain why I'd gone to such a bad college, or could sip some turned wine without flinching, or would know what drug slang meant in an arthouse addiction movie. We had met at twenty-six as Americans vacationing in Rome, passing down the stairs from the umbrella pines at the top of the city to the travertine arches over the gold-green Tiber. As a couple we were best when explaining something together, an idea or a poem, and could laugh until tears, holding each other's elbows, about a faux pas or malapropism. The remark I had made in my failing French: *Hitler and Stalin were one big problem*. The time at a lake in Slovenia when Greg hardly glanced over his shoulder where I pointed, to a fire in a drum metal trash can, and the cavalier way he rebuffed it—*Typical Slavic grill*—right before some of the burning garbage exploded. He'd grown up wealthy, which made me feel his choosing me was a greater compliment, but the way my poverty came up began to be a problem for him. He wanted to be alone together, to have pulled me cleanly from my life into ours. I still don't know if that was unfair, only that most facts of his background were not things he felt hunted by, and from which he had to cower, or stand up to shoot.

————————

The photos of us I reviewed without her: it was a ritual we typi-cally loved, Guin keeping a hand light on my back. She was comforted by the idea of a record, evidence that her life went on without her memory of it, and I was soothed by the proof of her *who*-lessness, how in one image she could give off many people—the floppy wave of a toddler, the blue stare of real age.

The day of that trip, we'd taken the 6 up from Civic Center to Golden Gate Park, where vanished, gray-complected men my parents might have partied with, still known as Fuzzy Bear and Socrates and Hazy Davy, mumbled as they sold most of everything for next to nothing. Those boomers were like the park's cyprus trees to us, everywhere you looked, as lifeless and as pissed-upon. There's a photo of Guin, euphoric right after we scored, going down the nearby concrete slides—an oddity in design that requires filthy playground sand in the descent, to create speed, and pieces of cardboard you ride down, gripping either side.

The day itself became a segmented spectacle, clearly divided into different situations and the feeling they radiated. I love boundaries like that—clean transitions. We peaked on the bus ride back to town, filling with anxious laughter we felt bounce down the aisle of the bus, and by the time we deboarded we weighed nothing, and were no one. Peta-luma was still made up of forgotten sheds, barns meeting little beaches of scrubs and anise, and we spent a little lifetime in the grass by the abandoned Ghirardelli factory on the water, believing the river was not reflecting pink light but producing it. We needed to be free and outside on those drugs, because of how they could flip your senses—leaves could chirp, light could drip—and work a similar inversion on your life, a punch line you might hear and laugh at but soon forget. *Well, I can't speak for myself,* I panted after a silence, facedown in cool dirt to quiet the colors, fucking up the idiom, and we laughed for a year. Sometimes you make a mistake and it feels like a blessing: lucky and funny: clear and perfect: so much purer than anything you could contrive.

When we'd come down enough that buildings no longer felt vicious, we went to visit Tim at the bar where he newly had a job. Depending on the drugs he didn't mention, and I never saw him use—was he smoking meth, shooting speed?—he could drink to shouting, captious oblivion or down a twelve-pack with no sign of it. He spent his shifts reading, Tom Robbins novels and histories of ancient civilizations, sagas and victories that played in the caves of his face. The swirls and spikes of his hair seemed like an expression of his intelligence. He'd been accepted to Berkeley but refused to pay for an education he could give himself, a fact most of his conversations eventually included. He had the kind of fine, aquiline face I saw later in sculpture halls, the Gen X slouch that went with their coffeeshop sofas. Tim could be useful and charming, playing us Psychic TV records and asking what we thought, taking us, when he had a car, out to the ocean, where he made a game of running up the high dunes—surprising us with a kite he'd had hidden in his jacket, or reciting the bit of Eliot he had memorized. Maybe it wasn't as much his age that was thrilling but his generation, the art they'd made of the T-shirt, the masterpiece of wasting time.

Guin had been sleeping with him on and off for eight months. Sometimes he seemed to worship her, and sometimes he disappeared, and there'd come a tight coil of days in which Guin was always in my bed, asking anxious, funny questions in the middle of the night. *Darlin', when you finish school could we get a little house out down D Street, and have some chickens and sell the eggs? Do those Ren fair girls think owning a lute is the same as having a personality? Are you sleeping? How old were you when you spelled your own name?* During those sleepovers we'd roll around cackling, doing impressions of people we hated, pretending to fart into the other's bare ass. Even my teeth wanted to fuck her. I could never decide if she wanted that, too, or if both of us did, whether it was for the wrong reason—that we'd shared everything else. The idea of there being some sound we'd never heard the other make, some face we'd never seen that meant *exactly that*, was as illogical as the fact we'd soon parcel our lives apart.

Hurrying back to my bed on one of these nights in the winter, having gone out in the ten p.m. rain to the store that took our IDs, we found Tim in the empty town plaza. He stood under an awning in a thermal and shower sandals, making the kind of snort he did at a dumb remark, over and over—except there was no remark, just the world around him. I felt Guin's hand clench where I held it. His eyes opened and closed, opened and closed, seeming to rinse almost greener. It was as if the simple fact of us offended him. How could we have been there, went the blink of his tic, when he was somewhere fucking else? There was a string of screaming cursing, nasal and elated, and when Guin said, *Let's go,* and took my elbow to walk on, he had followed us up some stairs and half a block, shouting and laughing for a terrible minute. Then he saw a left turn that somehow reconfigured him—he made a noise of recognition and disappeared without a word.

Guin wouldn't discuss it when I brought up these episodes later, acting like I'd violated his privacy. I didn't consider how he must have treated Guin's blackouts with the same hushed acceptance. *Respect comes in where love should be,* I read once in Tolstoy, stopping to underline it, thinking that distinction would be easy to see.

———————

Guin and I saw each other only once in our twenties, at the grocery store where she had taken a job bagging—I saw her, actually, apron clutched in her fist as she cleared the magazine rack by the bathrooms, not looking back long as she called goodbye to a coworker. Had she seen me where I stood in line? I was twenty-four, and fooling people in medical school with the silk shirts I hand-washed in my bathroom sink, a change in the way I pronounced *either* and *neither,* and I reasoned it was possible she hadn't recognized me. She'd gotten sober for the first time a few years before, and I knew she had suddenly married, an ex-con line chef—she'd worn celery-green to the city hall wedding, I saw on Facebook. Other than that she never posted, and sometimes I tried to google her, pulled my phone out and typed *Guin di Salvo Petaluma*, as though she were an unusual domestic problem, and I expected the internet to tell me what to do, to hear from people similarly afflicted. Her life was never online in the way mine was—just those creepy aggregators of phone numbers and addresses. She had so many, over the years.

Crossing through the grocery store parking lot a minute later, I watched her get into her husband's car. Standing on that same concrete, we'd once run into a former friend of mine, Sophie, who was star of symphony and debate, and she had sneered with rich concern. *Um, have you ever considered just coming to school?* Guin's answer came easily, in the same breath she took me by the waist. *Um, Sophie? Have you ever considered just furiously masturbating?*

As Guin and her husband roared by I was ready to wave, but her face was pitched down. It seemed to me he'd hit the gas before she'd even closed the door.

The photos of us blitzed and senseless I left scattered across the kitchen table, some dare for my mother to find, and then I read away the afternoon. Guin showed up drunk two hours later, announcing her arrival by pitching her bag through my open bedroom window, reorganized under an idea she'd had about what we should do. *About what?* I said, as she took off her shoes and socks, making a grotesque face at her own smell, then leaning one cheek to the cool promise of the wall. She made a snapping gesture at the bag, blitzed enough that the pads of her fingers barely made a sound, and I threw it at her harder than was necessary. Moving a hand through loose tobacco and coins and fireworks, ChapStick and condoms and shoe glue, she took out the envelope of photos, and I saw a new little tear at its fold.

Pointing at the neat capitals where Mr. Jones had written his contact information, a yahoo email address, Guin told me to get out my computer. I bet his AIM is the same, she said, crawling into my bed with splayed limbs. *Take off your jeans*, I said, *they're filthy*. She did, then held them way above her, grinning, poking her head through the two legs. Guin created a new account and added him to the buddy list, and then we waited, watching the videos we often did, as we swilled the bottle she'd brought. Again we laughed at Kelsey Grammer walking right offstage during a talk, James Brown calling into a news show hammered, saying, *I feel good!* in answer to every serious question, allegations of domestic abuse. These were our favorites: a man falling, a man refusing to fall. Would we have enjoyed these clips if they featured important women? I don't know, just that in the first grainy iteration of the internet they did not exist, and this only followed the pattern of the world we knew, triumphs and losses occurring mostly on the male side of things. There were clips of women stumbling and tripping, pert meteorologists accidentally drawing cocks that crossed oceans, but they were almost always anonymous— matronly or preadolescent shapes to be known only for the comical errors they made. When the sound came that meant a buddy had appeared online, Guin grabbed for my computer, roughly pressing the screen way back to squint at it. *Hey*, I said, *that cost money.* The alert was just our weed dealer, and I took the laptop back and primly shut it. *That lady could be in real trouble*, Guin said. *That man could be hurting her. Why aren't you worried about her?*

Because of her face in the fucking photos, I could have said. Because sometimes a small insult pays insurance against a larger, I wouldn't have thought yet, because maybe to be primitive for an hour a day is to be in control for the rest. Instead I asked a vicious question, one I sensed she wouldn't remember fielding anyway. She'd already dropped her bag onto the porch and put one leg out the window, and I propped myself up in my bed. *Are you trying to tell me Tim loves you while he fucks you?*

Guin returned to my bed, briefly, mounting me on my hipbones. *Give me your hand*, she said, laughing, and then she spit in it, smoker-thick and wet, closing my fingers onto my palm. *You're gonna learn so much at school.* I cried in the half hour after she left, loud enough that my mother came tentatively to my door and I sent her away, barking only, *Why is it so fucking hot in this house?* Except on the rare night a high temperature lasted into evening, she had the habit of moving the thermostat up to sixty-eight at night, saying the fog in early morning came in a cold draft. She was a thin, mysterious person, always putting on another sweater, never going farther than her ankles into the chilly ocean, smiling when I begged as a child for her to come, waving and saying she loved to watch me. By the time it was just the two of us I despised her caution, that aversion to the outside air. I would open all the windows and smoke her cheap cigarettes, shrugging when she cursed her empty pack the next morning, saying maybe she should quit.

I'm sorry, I T9'd Guin that night. *I love you. You're right. Let's make that man afraid of himself.*

———

When I heard about Guin's marriage—he had hit her a few times, she had left him, my mother saw his mug shot online—I felt a real victory for her, then something too close to jealousy. There was no good reason for what had happened between Greg and me: why he'd started sneering if I asked if he'd like to take a bath, walk and see the full moon, why I'd become some corrupt guard assigned to his life alone, asking what that look meant, that gesture, that pause, waking him in the morning to continue the argument. I would hear him brag about me to other people, and I praised him often, too, but in private he'd do and say things that I still can't unsee or unhear. Their cruelty was almost hidden, almost elegant. *I think you talk about your childhood for the attention, darling*, he'd say calmly, *but you already have mine.* One spring he stopped wanting sex, would shade his eyes if he saw me coming naked from the shower, or wince if I squeezed him in the kitchen. By summer he'd moved to the guest room, asking politely for my help in hanging some new art there. Often, I couldn't help it, I'd appear in his doorframe to beg and weep. *Oh, here's the quixotic quack again*, he liked to say, rolling his eyes, often in the same gesture he reached for his clean, warm handkerchief.

After he was gone, I wanted friends to say about my

husband what people must have about Guin's, that he was
a bad man, or that it was something else, the drug he loved,
which made him hurt her. But Greg stacked his books so
neatly when he left: he looked only like himself in his old
maroon sweater, crossing the lawn to his truck until the
boxes were loaded. There was his pageboy bob I'd loved, his
high rower's ass I used to hold in the shower. We'd been married by that pond, we'd run through that house, yelling some
news that would make the other laugh. And all anyone could
say, bored with my wretched mourning, was that he had been
a person.

———

I tried to get Guin alone, the few days after she'd slammed my
window shut, but she was always at Tim's apartment. It was a
top-floor one-bedroom he took great pride in, regaling us often
with battles he waged against his landlord. *That motherfucker,*
he would say, *is dealing with somebody who knows his rights as a
renter.* After Guin had turned me down twice for whiskey by
the river, I agreed when she invited me to his place, though I
had sworn myself against it. The last time I'd gone, I'd refused
to join them in the shower, and Tim had mocked my weak
explanation. *I'm really already clean,* I had said.

I stood there knocking a long time before they let me in. It
was seven p.m., and I had passed by windows where families
were just sitting down to dinner, fathers standing over tables
with large serving spoons, children unfolding blue napkins.
Tim kept his door locked and dead-bolted, and when Guin

finally opened it, wearing a black lace bra and grass-stained jeans, she looked damp and peaceful. In his room he kept a bed on a low imitation-wood frame, and in the kitchen a pool table. He'd been teaching Guin to play, all that spring and sum-mer, and she took to it naturally, sliding the cue behind her back as if it were a part of her body. She was good at everything process-oriented she tried, tools and games and diagrams—that year she'd built a solar panel, taught herself fifty birdcalls.

The moment I was inside, Guin crawled back into bed with him, where he lay smoking and holding a beer on his bare chest. They were so far in their drunk they'd turned placid and kind, Tim telling me there were Chinese leftovers in the fridge if I was hungry, Guin asking from her place on his shoulder what the weather had done all day. I gestured to a glass quart of tequila on the floor and began to catch up. When I asked Guin if she'd told Tim about the photos, she made a strange face, as if this were not the time—then, seeing his interest, she laughed and produced them. *If anyone deserves to be fucked*, she slurred as he flipped through, *it's that serious prince of a dog.* It was my thought that we call Mr. Jones, but I used words like *somebody*, playing in the hypothetical realm of juvenile humor. *Somebody should call him*, I said, *and tell him the police have the photos? Like the clerk reported them?* Tim spread them in a careful grid across the peaks and valleys of the unmade bed, chin tucked into his hand like the scientist he might have become. *Oh, so they were maybe in my class at Berkeley*, I remember him saying.

I saw the suggestion as airy and unreal, only something to feel better for joking about—but Tim lived beyond that, in the place of real rent and real anger, and soon was dialing the number on speaker. The moment rippled in a sensation I remembered from childhood, of a secret feeling exposed by adult force. The malt ball I'd stolen from the plastic grocery bin, rich and perfect in my cheek: lost to the trash can as my mother demanded, replaced by mealy shame. Guin leaned back on the bed behind where he sat up, saying we should talk about it first. She called him *honey* then, something I hadn't heard and that made me look at her another way. In it was a wish for peace that was nowhere in how she held her body, the muscled shoulders that appeared to meet the wind before the rest of her. Guin and I exchanged a look as he started to speak, something like a man as he first enters you, that tentative question of cruelty or kindness—*Will I hurt you or love you*, their faces always seem to say, *or is there something in you that might allow me both?*

Once he was really going, Guin wouldn't look at me, just started to press her splayed feet into the curve of his back. I could tell she was deepening the pressure there the more he refused to acknowledge it with any kind of glance back or touch, hinting at the kick that lived somewhere within her. Guin reached for the bottle between Tim's legs, trying thinly to get in the spirit of things. For a second she seemed like she might smile, looking like someone gamely following a story spoken in another language—only a thought behind at first, but soon dissociated from it entirely.

Yes, am I speaking with Matthew Jones? we heard him say, sensed the pause and the assent. The voice he used was one he hadn't around me, clear and clipped. *This is Lieutenant O'Reilly down here at the Petaluma Police Department. I'm calling about some photos you took, reported by a concerned citizen. That's right. Well, my first question, sir, and pardon my impertinence I think is the word, but is that your wife in those photos, or another consenting party? I see. And do you have any way of proving that?*

The man's faltering equivocations came in a rush, making amendments as they went. *We were enjoying ourselves privately,* Mr. Jones said, *and as far as I'm aware that's perfectly legal, but I'm, uh, of course happy to help clear up any misconceptions, Officer, truly sorry for any alarm.* Tim went on to clarify that, because of Mr. Jones's status as an educator in town, the department had a policy in place for anything untoward. However Guin or I had imagined Mr. Jones, cold with control, smooth with luck—he was something else on that call, namely uncertain about which part of his life he was meant to insist. The honor of his wife? The law as he knew it? The meaning of his privacy? The goodness of his heart?

Guin made a noise, a horsey exclamation from her fat, pursed lips, and Tim shot his hand back to cover her mouth. I could tell she was tonguing his palm, and in retaliation he tightened his grip and pinched her nipple, once, moving the phone away from his face to giggle. I hated them and I hated everything around them, the butts wilted in glass, the condom wrappers blooming on the wood crate that was the bedside table. *Is your wife at home, sir? Of course you'll understand I'll need her to tell me she was absolutely complicit. If you'd prefer, I can come down there, have a talk on the porch.*

No, Guin said, into Tim's fingers. *Stop it.*

Fucking prank, we heard Mr. Jones say in the background. *Probably. Small town. I don't know, to be sure* . . . And then there was his wife's voice, calmer than his, saying something like, *Let me take care of it.* Mrs. Jones spoke her name firmly, sincerely, and I watched the sound of it pass over Tim's face. He hadn't planned that far, or had only expected to move against her resistance—only to mock these people in an underhanded advance against their bigger part of the world. Saying something specious about protocol, spewing bullshit numbers, naming a bullshit code, Tim asked whether the gag in her mouth was definitely what she wanted. *Are we done?* she said.

It was clear then that the woman had never believed his lie. Understanding this, Guin's eyes were filling as she pressed her fingernails into her temples. She curled her toes into Tim's back. Before she erupted—would she cry, would she hit?—there were always signs like this, her insides protesting their limits. She lived in her body as some people live in temporary housing. Unsure how long the arrangement will last, they ruin the walls with holes and marks, they slam the cheap doors. Tim began to speak in the high shriek I'd heard that misting night we'd run into him, adding an affected babying lisp. *Do you hate your yuppie life so much that having your gerbil of a husband tie you up was the only way to come?*

Guin was on top of Tim then and slapping his ears, trying to wrest the phone away for a long time after the Jones household had gone silent. *Fucking stop it*, Guin kept saying, for too long after he had. As the phone fell from his hand and his giggle accelerated, I grabbed my jacket and pulled it around my sweatshirt, leaving his door unlocked. My hood was up against a thick mist as I walked home, and I felt glad to be obscured. I knew how soon I would pay for misunderstanding what Guin needed: To feel righteous about a crime that didn't involve her, but was hers to define. To fantasize inviolably, and indefinitely, about some justice only she could dispense.

————

I stopped going back to Sonoma County, in part because it lost its weather—I used to love that drizzle and fog, but now it only floods or catches fire. Guin and I spent a decade angry at each other, but the year we were twenty-eight we returned to our friendship and confessed. She had found my email online and sent me one rich in her singular misspellings, telling me only a little about the husband or the heroin, which always went unnamed. There'd been *hard work and a little bit of luck*, she said, but now! She was clean. She was new. We talked about Suboxone and her first-ever bout as a single person, the audiobooks she loved on politics and psychology, the granny unit she had triumphantly rented a few towns over from Petaluma, despite bad credit and an eviction and a mug shot on her record. Once a month, for most of six, we'd Skype—the internet was another one now, capable of bringing our lives closer together, but still faulty enough her face might slow down, her language stop. *I don't know what happened*, I notice everyone always rushing to say, just as Guin and I did, returning to each other after a connection drops. Why? Don't we know exactly what happened, that the version of intimacy made possible by twitching screen is improbable to begin with? That if you know behind you is the safety or danger of your own life, that if you can't smell someone starting to sweat, or see the way they curl their fingers when they mention a certain person's name, the version you get and give can't really be trusted?

That's what happened with Guin and me, ultimately. During a conversation that was creaking anyway—she seemed far away as she was, and answered most questions about the past few weeks with a limited set of *Good, Okay,* and *Not the best*— her face poured into bits. Two minutes later, she took advantage of the conversation restarting to ask about me. Were my patients behaving themselves? As I began to describe a client's unique delusion, Guin's husband called her name, and then he moved on-screen to kiss her forehead. *Anything from the store, babe?* She blushed deeply, saying something quickly about smokes, and sent him away.

We were silent a long time, the country between us redrawing our faces in pixelated revolutions if she shifted or I did. She apologized first for the state of the connection, saying the internet was bad in what she called *west county.* They'd gotten back together a few months before, she admitted, when they both were sober, and I knew, I knew, I *knew* by the way her glance fell that they were no longer. He'd been living there and they were doing sobriety together, she said, hoping I'd say something accepting—but I had returned to who I'd become again, and I refused even to ask how long.

The lie had been as beautiful as she still was, but I'd forgotten how she smelled, that she was handy with a pocketknife—the time she had, with loving conspiracy, convinced a waiter to send a crying child a milkshake in an IHOP. Devotion rarely goes on without novel surfaces, isn't that right? Without the grain of new situations it can be confirmed against. Greg, when I told him about the call, nodded in sympathy. He scrounged up some stained little words that we've all, in selfishness, used. *There is only so much you can do.*

It's funny he could say that when he'd heard the sound I'd made, on that call, when I saw the face of her husband. I cried out in the way I do when I see a cockroach, as though it's the first time and I haven't been living all my life in these fucking American houses, built quickly of pest-friendly wood. If you get from one side of this country to the other, or the bottom to the top, you find out that even the wealthy are living in buildings that were not meant to last, and that the American imagination is selfish and short, and that the shrug we give when someone else needs something is a consequence of how long our memory is, and how far we can see into the future—and the answer to all of it is, well, about a hundred years. That's how long the walls will stand if you do nothing, and that's also the scope of history you're expected to know or care about. It's a friendly, easy figure because it stretches just about one life, indicating any person's decades as an exception, not a pattern. There are accidents of passion, here, not designs of cruelty. And so we go around chirping, *Life is short!* which is a way of saying, *My life is mine!* which is a way of saying, *Best of luck with yours!*

———————

Greg moved out just before the virus, actually—I don't even have that to blame. In the first six months of it, I seemed to spend my sadness only on my friends' and clients' lives, laughing at the right moments, adjusting their medications, often avoiding the diagnoses that would do little to help them and everything to set them against me. You tell a person they're a recognizable type, you call a symptom specific to a pattern of others, and they're likely to rage or turn mute. Few of us want to believe that our pain is so common it can be treated.

In my personal life anyway, I've tried to select against certain categories, and never got it quite right. Greg had accepted exactly one drink in his life—his father was an alcoholic, too—and I'd *chosen* his sobriety, his pellucid memory. Living with him, I learned his religious tidiness, to empty rooms in order to sweep them. *Oh love*, he had said, laughing, our first apartment together, looking at my dishes as he washed them, *would you let me teach you?* I was then twenty-six, and the undersides of my pots all looked almost caramelized. *How funny that you never*, Greg said, kissing me, *learned to wash the bottoms of things.*

He was careful and tender with all his senses, coming home with dark chocolate and olive oil soap in his tote bag, straightening the rooms we slept in so that nothing bigger ever sat on anything smaller, and all the angles were right. But once he was unhappy, his tongue seemed to fatten with another decade, and his pupils expanded, as he stayed up all night reading the internet, until his brown eyes seemed only to be black. He had the snap of a drunk, the lurching impulses that hated to be seen. Toward the end I woke once, frightened, around three a.m., to the bed frame vibrating with a deep, frantic bass, Mahler's fifth booming from his office speakers a floor below. As if I were his neighbor, I knocked timidly, asking that he might turn that down. And he stomped across the room, slamming a hand down to quiet the noise, his eyes flashing that deep black and holding mine. He would say things I imagined had been once said to him (*Do you think you're the first person to suffer?*) or pose a mean, specific question (*You never got over your father dying, did you?*) and behave with no memory of it the next day, when I might find him whistling as he cleaned the kitchen, or arranging narcissi in my office with a lucky wink. Even as they horrified me, I envied him those outbursts. Because the worst things I've said or done, and the worst said and done to me, have worked on my life more quietly, like some embarrassing, insuperable superstition—keeping me from walking where it must be safe to, assuring me I know something other people don't.

———————

I waited an hour on my porch for Guin, knowing she would come, thinking of the Jones house nearby—the dog who might be passing from room to room, wondering about the change to the way his people were speaking, the lights maybe not turned on at dusk. Through the walls behind me was the bed where I slept, the narrow corridor of sink and pantry where my mother drank her coffee alone by the small, high window. The unhappiness of my life in that apartment was perfectly tailored, shaped like the two of us, and I knew the unhappiness beyond would be a surprise for which I had no retort prepared.

When Guin showed up, I announced straightaway we would return the photos. She nodded and took the package from her bag, handing it to me with a look she must have learned in her childhood: Was her sin so bad? Would she be forgiven? I could see in the streetlight how battered it was, the photo on top of the pile a little bent at an edge. I didn't ask why the stack seemed slimmer, or about the tape she'd run on the envelope where it had torn, in some kind of apology. Even her anger she couldn't really care for, or be loyal to, in the way so many people do for the rest of their lives, using the same language to describe it. *My father's narcissism was one of small differences*, a client will tell me, again and again, seeming proud of their articulation. Whatever Guin's failings, she never gave me the same sentence twice.

———————

In college I didn't mention her, though I understood that I was desirable mostly because of the print she'd left on me. She had taught me how you remove a bottle cap with any edge, how you breathe around a cock in your mouth or run backward from a bottle rocket. *You're not going to be this sad your whole life*, she had said once in bed, holding me from behind, her ribs bigger than my ribs, her voice clearer than my voice, and

I knew it was something like an insult. She was standing at the perspective of distance between us she already saw. Even if I could drink to nothing with her, stay up on speed and get sliced to ribbons by hateful daylight, I eventually felt the need to return to myself. Faithful student I was at heart, I wanted the home in my mind that would ratify anything I'd done, convert it into some lesson or anecdote.

In the middle of my first semester of college, I heard from my mother that the Jones dog had gone missing. Flyers punctuated the neighborhood, using the word *love*, entreating the town's sympathy. My mother admitted to me she saw it—trotting downhill, one early morning she was half-asleep and smoking out front—but its beauty was such, its certainty so evident, that she could not stop to worry. From her voice on the phone, I understood that she knew this was wrong, how it's those creatures most easily alone you're supposed to call after as they run toward traffic.

Can you imagine losing your dog the same month you lost your job? she asked, but I wouldn't take the bait, wouldn't ask how or why. That was roughly the position I held on anything having to do with Petaluma, and that might be why we never really talked about the time after dad died, when she kept the apartment too warm and we'd acknowledge each other like roommates. Once, when she came to visit me and Greg, and he had slipped off to fix dessert, the topic did come up. Her thin hand grabbed for mine, and she smiled wetly in the sweet candlelight and mentioned those years and said, *Someday, babe, when we have a sign the time is right.*

I did tell a friend the full story of what we did to the Jones marriage, recently, during a series of Zooms about what she was willing to do for her husband's pleasure. With the pandemic on, they needed something new in their life, but it would have to be a compromise, she reiterated, and I agreed: he'd been watching the kind of *Down, sex-pig!* porn where women's makeup forms runnels down their alarmed faces, and she was interested in *shibari*, if she could get the right kind of silk ropes from Japan. The friend had been calling often, and I would allow her to repeat her banal remarks, or call me back when her contractor needed to run through something on her kitchen's renovation. Listening to my details of fifteen years before, she laughed at the mischief of it all, and repeated a line I sensed she had read on internet forums about that kind of sex. *Sometimes the bottom is the top.* Then she changed the subject.

It had been so nice to say Guin's name, but the friend had asked nothing further about her, who she had been to me or what she'd become to herself. The next time she texted I vanished the text, the next time she called I silenced the call, the next time she emailed I archived the email. I told myself I was bored by the conversation. False power, voluntary confinement, doesn't interest me. If you add it up, the leather with the lotion, the cruelty with the kindness, doesn't that only get you somewhere neutral? And that's worse than being alone—which I actually like fine—given the lie of being together.

All I had wanted, on that call, was the chance to say the outrageous, impossible words that had become true a few weeks before. It was the only conversation in which it would have been appropriate, because I had never really mentioned Guin to anyone else. She had existed before I became myself. It would anyway require so many steps down their empathic ladders, those lawyers and doctors, a series of bleak facts going lower and lower, deeper and deeper, and by the time I got to the phrase, they would have been worn out. Because first, I'd want to say how once she was sober again she realized her wisdom teeth had been so painful she'd had no choice but to pull them and that $2,000 was impossible . . . and so her landlord had cut off the electricity . . . and when the virus hit she was living in a trailer without water, which was meant to be temporary . . . she had a good job at a restaurant but all but two of the front of house staff were cut . . . and the NA meeting that was important to her didn't go digital, for some reason, and it felt wrong to start a new meeting on a screen, with intermittent Wi-Fi . . . and actually . . .

She died.

It was Tim who let me know, calling me on repeat from midnight in California, and I picked up in my sleep, as weak and confused as he must have remembered me. My terror, when I heard his voice, was so pure it touched everything—it made the rug I brought my feet onto rough, the books splayed all around me in my bed jagged and menacing. He said something first about Guin being the love of his life, testing out how it sounded. I could tell he was outside, and I remembered how natural he always looked near a streetlamp, as thin, and as cold, and as punitive.

There was no euphemism: Guin had not "passed on."
"Four milligrams of pure fucking fentanyl," he announced.
"She never did anything lightly, which I have to admit I fucking admire." That he and Guin had not talked in some seven
years, that he and I had not in fifteen, that she saw my life
as a put-on and I saw hers as a curse on mine—these things
weren't a part of the conversation. Shortly after relating some
gruesome details, he switched topics, but I was still thinking
about the week she'd been alone with her dead body, and only
vaguely registered what he said next. He had heard I'd become
a doctor, which didn't surprise him. He wanted to tell me about
a combination of *ingredients* he'd been using to treat a recur-
rent sinus infection—maybe we could talk, have a *meeting of
the minds*, get it on the shelves. I could feel myself readying the
condescending remark, that I was not that kind of doctor, that
he hadn't the right to . . . and then it drifted away, easily as an
hour does when you spend it lying down. I couldn't hold on to
my offense at his having called me, asking myself in the next
instant what I'd kept the same number for, if not this. You must
want to be reached, I told myself. You must need some part of
you that goes all the way back.

"Do you want to meet up?" Tim said. "A drink for the old
days." "Where are you?" I asked him, rather than answering
I was in Vermont. I was convinced, somehow, by the short-
circuiting of his mind. Even his ruined thinking was clever,
understanding that I had left and couldn't have really, daring
me to deny it.

"Downtown," he said, like the answer was obvious. I

clarified my location, apologizing, and he got off the phone soon after, pulling the phone away from his mouth to shriek, "Oh, is that fucking *right*," to something or someone I couldn't see. And then I knew it, certain as the draft through the bedroom window—that if he'd been three blocks away, that if I could walk to him, I would have, saving the buttoning of my coat for the walk through the weather.

————

The days or weeks after seem to fall down, their natural order like something you only narrowly catch, the save so close you've already imagined the irretrievable break. Some people go and you can't imagine the bridge, how their bodies went from being memories to being silence, but it wasn't difficult to picture Guin dying. She had practiced a long time. What bothers me about her death, the thought that cracks my chest open to a sob in the bulk food aisle, is that I believe it so easily I keep trying to remember it. That the last place she'd ever gone was one where we'd never been together—it's the force that holds me down in my bed until noon some mornings, and makes me wrench my stove from the wall to sweep behind it another.

The fentanyl I keep in my bedside drawer, for months after I hear about Guin, an insult to her, I know—that I got it easily and legally and paid nothing, that I can keep it hidden in a room where I read and clean, sleep and masturbate. *There is only so much you can do*, to use Greg's phrase, but in another selfish context—as in, only so much you can do of this drug, if you want to come back. The threshold is famous, the bottom.

I know I wouldn't have gotten it if he had still been nearby, in his tidy other bedroom, and also how lucky I feel to be alone with her—in my mind, I mean, in my body.

"I just think you're unwell," the client chirps again, how many sessions after the first time I can't truly say. "And I want you to know I respectfully decline the opportunity to work with you anymore." *You are the only one here*, the HIPAA-compliant digital office software informs me after that, so why do I stay there a moment longer, looking at the frame of my life as it's been presented? The window that's best for western light, the row of plants we all keep to remind ourselves of an outside. Then I float upstairs, thinking I'll get some laundry together, and I take a pill. It happens so easily: the idea of *once* has always seemed friendly. I could forgive anything in myself or in him, Greg liked to say, a compliment one day and an insult the next.

————

In the depth of August, Guin and I pass up quiet, sloping streets. Outside the Jones house we stop, maybe hoping to learn something about that man and that woman, but in their lit bedroom the curtains are drawn, and all we can understand is that they are together. I push the photos into the mailbox that stands on a post, and we continue up the hill to the park we like, situated high above the rambling town. From a damp bench we take in Petaluma, the enormous grain elevator and the purple hills occurring all around it.

You wanted to hurt them because they're lucky, I say to Guin, and the underside of that sentence is that there is nothing she could do to make her life like theirs, but there's plenty I could, and will. Guin cocks wide and clips short, and when I start to bleed from my top lip, when I feel the notch in my tooth where it will be forever, she laughs brightly as a toddler who has just understood that ice can melt, or green give way to blossom.

She doesn't tell me that Tim has taken some of the photos, and she can't know that a few weeks from now he'll be over at McNear Elementary in the middle of the night, supergluing them image-in to the tilt-and-turn fifties windows of the choir classroom. It's not her fault how the children who trot in on their first day of school will see those adult secrets, those strange expressions, as part of their view of outside, or that their teacher will seem scary as he tries to pick them off, cursing when he finds he can't cleanly detach one part of his life from another.

———

It's dark early in Vermont, and a sound is more likely to come from within the house than out, a faucet, a radiator. As for my life, I've got thick, hand-knit socks on, a full glass of cool water, and a third pill, now, another half a milligram: it's such a small thing against such a big house. Narcan in the drawer, she might have teased me for that, and fuck her. What did I owe her? A call every day? A check every month? A plane ticket would have been easy, an inpatient spell someplace else where her ex couldn't wait in the parking lot. I could have given an apology for her life, not because it was my fault, but because it should have been somebody's. In my bedroom the objects have been rearranged since Greg left, end tables and necklaces, oils and creams. There's the rug from Athens, the vase from Sausalito, another on my tongue, then a dull, happy truth. It makes my ribs bigger, lets each breath go farther.

I laugh when I know it! The absurdity in counting! *Six?* When was the last time you saw one in real life, a number? I can only speak for myself, but I *never* see a pretty wall of trees, or a stark impasse of mountains, and know there are twelve. No one *ever* goes on loving someone because it's been so many years. They might just be a category, numbers, something that helps other people understand what we don't need to.

Somewhere under the covers, somewhere under my mind, we snake our way through town in the middle of the night, up and down the gravel of those little alleys, named *School* and *Telephone* and *Pepper*, seeing into the backsides of magnificent houses. *Half-gabled, cross-timber.* She's learned to describe the homes of other people, faithful and tender as the owners must be, pointing with her chin tucked on my neck. *Frieze, coffer.* I kiss her for knowing, I adore her again, she walks deep into shadow, I go deep in my body, lick my tooth where she's chipped it, she forgives us all distance, we come from the same place, we are parts of the same life.

Maybe we aren't girls, surely we were never children, but we might have the talents of animals, sensing everything that wants to kill us, and that we need to kill. Hills aren't a problem, gates we can perch on, dark we can see in, and now we're quiet by the glow of that couple's back window. What's the ancient idea, we've read it somewhere, we turn in the chilly bed to find it, we turn her face in the light of other lives to tell her. We're born knowing everything, which is why we wail. We begin to forget, which is how we can stop. And here's the thing: here's the thing: here's the strangest, loving thing, which helps until it doesn't, which is kind until it's wicked:

At the end of your life, you've forgotten the most.

ACKNOWLEDGMENTS

♦

READERS (in order)

John Wray,[1] Jin Auh and Charles Buchan,[2] Matt Dojny, Alexandra Kleeman, Valeria Luiselli, Corinna Barsan, Jesse Ball, Halimah Marcus, Sally Rooney, Catherine Lacey, Ross Scarano, Alex Ross Perry, Manuel Gonzales, Farhad Mirza,[3] Annabel Davis Goff,[4] Jonathan Ames, Smith Henderson

MANAGEMENT

Bill Clegg[5] and Simon Toop

INSTITUTIONS, EDITORS, AND PUBLICATIONS

Katie Ryder at *Harper's*; Michael Dumanis at *The Bennington Review*; Michael Ray at *Zoetrope*; MacDowell; Anthony Doerr and Heidi Pitlor for *Best American Short Stories*; Lauren Groff and Jenny Minton Quigley

---

[1]   Thank you for what you gave my sentences those years.

[2]   You each urged my earliest attempts in this form toward clarity and muscle: I am so grateful.

[3]   Emergency contact is correct. How lucky I am to know you.

[4]   Just to flay this horse, you changed most of everything.

[5]   There is my career before you came on, then my career after; thank you for calling early and late to gossip about suffering and the fouetté to the preterite; I am more than fortunate and no less than indebted.

for the O. Henry Prizes; Columbia University; Bennington College; Erin Sinesky Lovett, Drew Weitman, and Jill Bialosky at W. W. Norton

EXTERNAL

Robert Harbison, Joann Callis, Nan Goldin, Marsden Hartley, The Beach Boys, Genesis P. Orridge, Ben Young's *Hounds of Love*, Virginia MacAlester, Shulamith Firestone

PLACES

Provini, The Odeon, Walter's, Big Bar, The Whitney, Film Forum, and IFC Center in New York; The Dresden Room in Los Angeles; The American Legion Post 82 in Nashville; the Serpentine Gallery at Hyde Park in London

OTHERS WHO LOVED, AFFIRMED, ENCOURAGED, FED, DROVE, OR HOUSED ME IN 2016–2023

Connor Yorke Martin, Larry Krone, Dan Olincy, Johnson Henshaw, Michael Masterson, Michael Stamm, Michelle Shofet, Micah Gordon and Daniel Kaufman,[6] Esme Shapiro, Jess Brownell, Jason Porter and Shelly Gargus, Tony Michael Presley, Catherine Ball, Sheila Imandoust and Robbie Simon, Barry and McLean Benjamin, Lisette Vega and Michael Hammer, Matthieu Aikins, Phil Coldiron, Cassie Waddell and Gabriel Magaña, Jesse Thurston, Benjamin Brewer, Nathan Reese and Connie Wang, Alexis Mitchell, Ross Mann[7]

---

[6]   I think of you in the same breath, as in: if there have been more devoted and brotherly friends, I assume they have neglected all other obligations and are living in ruin.

[7]   What a masterpiece of tenderness you have become. Thank you for putting my sense of my fiction, and my fiction about my life, upright.